CARELESS

CARELESS

JANE FOSTER

GREEN DRAGON BOOKS

Green Dragon Books
Palm Beach, Florida, USA

Green Dragon Publishing
P.O. Box 1608
Lake Worth, FL 33460
http://www.greendragonbooks.com
info@greendragonbooks.com

Printed in the United States of America and the United Kingdom

ISBN (Paperback) 978-1-62386-054-7
ISBN (e-book) 978-1-62386-055-4

Library of Congress Cataloging-in-Publication Data Control # Available

As always to my precious children with all my love

ACKNOWLEDGMENTS

I love having this opportunity to thank all my family and friends who listened, read, gave me their expertise and encouraged me during the writing of CARELESS.

Each of you made a difference. I want to thank my cousin and dance impresario, Tom Flagg, choreographer and dancer, Demetrius Klein, and editor and friend, Gretel Furner for the generous sharing of their knowledge and time. I also want to thank Anne and Richard Yelland, Giraud Lorber, Augusta Lorber, Rob Reid, Donna Casey, Dr. Heath King, Patricia Hilton, Virginia Swift, Susan Gubelmann, Sally Ohrstrom, Kathy Snowden, Della O'Donahue, Cole Myers, Ann Copeland, Stephan de Angeles, Victoria Hagerty, Barbara Lambesis, Peyton Bruns, Susan Ramsay, Helen Pilkington, Pat Durkin, Sheila Shane, Helen Emanuel, Lynn Hightower and the amazing Sally Johnson.

CHAPTER ONE

For many years, Charlotte Darling, principal dancer for New York City Ballet, had been faithful to Cheetos and M&Ms, even while dieting, but recently she'd forsaken Valium for Xanax. The daily flight from reality to euphoria was taking longer than usual, and this morning, as she lay in bed watching the video of a recent rehearsal, she pressed pause and allowed time to hang heavily on her hands.

Charlotte never touched alcohol nor smoked anything other than fine Virginia tobacco, so she added another Xanax to the previous two and waited for her memories to improve. Rearranging memories in order to record them as they certainly should have been was how she spent her time now. The irritating fact that these did not necessarily correspond to Colin or Lilly or Topsy's memories didn't seem to bother her. She liked them just the way she typed them out in Word.

Charlotte's Web. She wanted to call it *Charlotte's Web*. God knew she'd woven it and repaired every gash with the glittering thread of her fame. But that title was already taken. Perhaps, *Charlotte's Dance*. God knew she'd danced. Danced on the great stages all over the world—Lincoln Center in New York, the Garnier in Paris, the Mariinsky in St. Petersburg, and so many others. Her autobiography could run five hundred pages or more if it included copious photographic evidence of her beauty and success, but there was much she didn't want to revisit. Right now she'd lie back on this great pile of goose down pillows and let the relative silence of Saturday morning in New York City slide through the open window with the crisp October air. She'd relax now and think about things later.

Later came suddenly with the phone jangling next to her head. The high-pitched whine of her daughter Topsy's voice was infinitely distressing.

She put the phone on speaker and lit a cigarette. She blew the smoke high over her head and watched as it disappeared into the canopy, which she noticed was no longer white. Nicotine had yellowed it along with her unpolished nails. Her teeth, though, were startling in their whiteness.

"Stop, Topsy," she said and replaced the receiver on the white plastic cradle.

Charlotte's feelings of guilt were still confused and complex, her body still strong and light. Her raven hair was streaked with gray and was kinkier than she remembered it being when she was younger, even when wet with sweat. But in those days, it was strictly pulled back and constrained in a tight bun, flaunting her chiseled features. Now it lay loose and long and disheveled on the rumpled pillowcase.

She continued sucking the noxious smoke deep into her powerful lungs and tried to pinpoint when her life took the wrong turn. Memories tumbled through her mind until they landed on a moment three years earlier, which seemed a likely point.

The shit storm started when I broke my shoulder, she thought. That, as everyone knows, was all Colin's fault. In fact, everything that's gone wrong was all Colin's fault. How could a househusband, like him, with a degree from the London School of Economics, sanction a mess like this, she wondered? Well, maybe 'sanction' was a bit rich, but it happened on his watch and in his area of expertise. Admittedly, the degree was only a Bachelor of Science, earned by correspondence, but she'd never asked much of him. After all, she was the one who had to train, rehearse, perform—maintain the image. *And* publicly relate at all times and in all places as directed by exacting experts. She made *all* the money, but he was supposed to keep it safe.

Oh, and yes, she thought, I must continue to be the flawless hostess, producing frequent events, you could hardly call them parties anymore, in Palm Beach, Newport and here in New York for French perfumers, Italian shoemakers and American pharmaceutical executives as well as visiting performing artists. With whatever time there might be left over, Charlotte had to entertain the press and try to be a good mother, wife, sister, daughter, employer, dancer and friend. For God's sweet sake, couldn't he keep the money safe?

Colin, the finance man. What can she say? She guessed she could flatter him and write about how he took my modest inheritance from Dad and made it into . . . wait a minute. What did he make it into? Zero. At best. And now he's gone and lost the massive proceeds from Prima. Prima, the world's best-selling perfume, and all the licensing dough for the ballet flats and sneakers.

Thank God bleached and brilliantly capped teeth continue to fascinate the toothpaste-buying public, and luckily Charlotte's were America's favorite set. Where would they be without those bracing checks every quarter? And what about the money made from the sweat off her back, she wondered? There'd be nothing to sell if she hadn't done all that sweating.

Somehow all her work was not enough to make up for Colin. Whatever could have made him do such an idiotic thing? She preferred to think it was an impulse rather than willful malfeasance or something incurable, like stupidity. Still, she could kill him for putting all the eggs in one basket. And let it be noted, she laid each and every egg without any help from him. Isn't it Economics 101? Always inspect basket before putting eggs in, never put too many eggs in one, and check with goose who lays golden eggs before making big egg decisions. Surely, that's what's taught in every business course.

Now she owns optics. But not optics to improve vision. Optics for security. I'd like to meet the schemer who convinced Colin that his scanner, now *her* scanner, would be in every security checkpoint on this planet and beyond. She wanted to meet him and spit in his eye.

Charlotte lit another cigarette and reveled in hate. Hatred directed mainly at Colin, but some seeped out towards faceless others involved in her financial debacle. The sheer magnitude of her animosity gave her a thrill. The passion it evoked was strong, something like love. Lilly told her she could choose—she could stop blaming him or call the cops. She said all this loathing was killing Charlotte and not hurting Colin one bit. Lilly was her manager, and younger sister, who knew it all. Charlotte didn't buy into any of Lilly's pseudo-psychology, though. She loved hating Colin and savoring all his infractions. She figured the comfort this provided must be closer to 'good' for her rather than 'bad'.

Lying quietly in her bed, she watched Colin's love affairs parade through her mind like Mardi Gras floats. She enjoyed having him in the dock of her imaginary courtroom, indicting him for crime after crime. And now with the optics outrage, she felt justified in cancelling the lease on his suite of offices on Madison Avenue. She wanted to have him at home. She liked hearing him walk on eggshells. Her eggshells.

The phone rang again. Grimacing, she reached for it. The screen read Lilly.

"What," she said.

"Topsy said you hung up on her."

"You people are so perfect all the time. Such an inspiration to me."

"She's your only child. I'd think you'd want to be less careless with the relationship."

"She's too expensive. I can't afford her anymore."

"You'll have a huge advance from Tandem Hall as soon as you give them a first draft."

"Why don't you write it then? Or better yet, Topsy. Miss English Lit."

"She just wants to finish her dissertation. You can afford her for another six months. All these economies were not part of her life-map."

"Her *life-map*? Give me a break." Charlotte took a satisfying drag on her Marlboro Red.

"You brought her up in the very lap of luxury and now you expect her to drop everything. Just like that. It's a bit much when you sit there at the top of 740 Park."

"Where do you want me to sit? Newport and Palm Beach are mortgaged to the hilt and the grounds have gone to hell. At least here, if I avoid the mirrors, I don't have to see the ruin of what was once so beautiful."

"God, Charlotte, you should listen to yourself. What's gotten into you? Or is it just another role?"

"So glad you think it's a role." Charlotte stubbed her cigarette out with a vengeance. "I've got to get back to my manuscript. So I can finance everyone."

"A lot of people have contributed to your success, and no one has more support troops than you do. Legions."

"I paid heavily for those 'contributions,' and the legions get weekly paychecks signed by me. As I've said before, you're welcome to write the whole goddamned autobiography, if you want to."

"I think it's time to start calling it a memoir."

"You can check that off your list of things I need to do. Tandem is fine with it being a memoir."

"I can't believe you're so bitchy today. Menopause? Or something more?"

Charlotte slammed the phone down for the second time that day. Cut them all off. She couldn't cope with the compounded self-hatred all this was causing her.

Chemical comfort was finally kicking in. Neural pathways were opening up the way she liked them. She pulled the computer onto her lap and opened up the document and started typing.

> "Two months after Topsy was born, the invitation came from Anthony Dowell, Director of the Royal Ballet, to dance Odette and Odile in *Swan Lake* with the fabled company at the Royal Opera House in Covent Garden! Ever since I was a tiny little girl, I'd modeled myself on Dame Margot Fonteyn, and now I was about to have three days of her undivided attention. And

> I'd dance on the very stage where she'd held London swooning at her feet for decades. This was the star-spangled stuff that my dreams were made of, and they were coming true! I took out my very special apple-green writing paper designed by Mrs. John L. Strong and replied to him, *'yes I said yes I will Yes'*. And sent it to London with two love stamps on the upper right-hand corner of the vibrant envelope."

I can hear Lilly reading this. Listening to her cynical voice in my head is ruining my writing. Nah, nah, nah, boo, boo. I'll write what I want to.

> "In May, Colin and I flew with Topsy and her nannies from New York to London on Concorde. We were met by a corps of VIPs and a large Rolls Royce. A three-bedroom suite was waiting for us at Claridge's. I could smell the lilacs the minute I stepped off the elevator. Huge bouquets of them with peach-colored roses and deep pink peonies were blooming on every flat surface. A magnum of Cristal was lounging in a silver bucket of ice. Charbonnel et Walker violet creams were stacked on tiered porcelain trays, and Floris reigned in the bathroom. I was in heaven. All my little girl dreams were coming true, and my own darling eight-month-old daughter and my treasured husband were there with me. We were a fairytale trio, adored by the press, the public and each other."

This is my memoir, Charlotte thought. Not Lilly's, nor Topsy's and certainly not Colin's. Readers don't care what any of them remember. She knew that trip was before the licensing money started flooding in and that the 'nannies' were her mother and Lilly. But if you asked her mother, she would only remember that Charlotte was not in prime form, four pounds over prime, to be exact. Colin would remember they were fighting. He claimed it was hormonal issues after Topsy's birth, conveniently forgetting about Allison and others. And Lilly would remember that she had to share a room with her mother. Anyway, the trimmings were fabulous and exactly as she described them.

CHAPTER TWO

Just after Charlotte was born, Roy and Kay Darling moved from Leesburg to Middleburg, Virginia. As soon as the budget allowed, they bought a sturdy little 19th century fieldstone farmhouse and hired a local socialite to decorate it with hunting prints and chintz. They wanted the right setting for Charlotte. Everything was done with her future in mind. Already, at two, anyone could see she was unusually coordinated and beautiful, and she always stole the show.

Roy was a good horseman and joined the posh Middleburg Hunt, blazing a trail for his daughter. Kay did not enjoy hunting. All that excited horse, dog and human flesh lusting for blood made her cringe with fear, rather than with disapproval. She didn't let Roy see she was afraid and often brought little Charlotte with her to see the hunt off. She always had a good excuse why she couldn't follow them. She'd let herself be persuaded to go on trail rides, though, but only ones that didn't require jumping over stone walls.

The Darlings were a contented threesome for five years, and Charlotte flourished, sandwiched as she was between two adoring parents. Roy gave Charlotte a pony for her third birthday. The pony, named Cocoa, was boarded at Nina Pipes' stable, less than a mile away. Nina had an outdoor riding ring and taught dressage to the neighborhood children three times a week, in all but the foulest weather. She was about the same age as the Darlings, but her poignant sadness and formal manner made her seem older. Kay was curious about Nina and found out from the local gossips that Nina, who was once considered the prettiest girl in Loudoun County, had been left standing at the altar by a green-eyed Irishman named Kevin McGettigan. The light went out of her eyes that day, and less than a year later her only sibling was one of the first American casualties in Vietnam.

Nina's smiles were reserved for children. She loved the horses, though, and could be heard singing as she groomed them daily. She rode to hounds on Mondays and Thursdays from the first day of cub hunting in early September through the last fox hunt in mid-March. Otherwise, she could be found in the stables or at Covert, her family's red brick house, about a hundred yards down a path winding through an apple orchard. Nina was the only one left in her immediate family and lived alone, rarely inviting anyone over the age of twelve through the front door.

It was a disappointment for Kay to find she was expecting another child. But Roy was delighted, and his delight infuriated Kay. She wanted him to be as complete with three as she was. Lilly didn't know her mother and sister were not happy to see her on the day she was born. What the whole county knew was how proud her father was. He did the old-fashioned thing of giving out cigars to all and sundry to celebrate the joyous event of little Miss Lillian's birth. They named her after his mother, who was always known as Lilly.

Roy Darling might have become a rich and famous oilman. He was a wildcatter and had drilled one exceptional well. But when Lilly was three weeks old and the day after Charlotte's fifth birthday, he lost his life on a rig in the Gulf of Mexico. That day a storm blew in out of nowhere and a rogue wave claimed him at age thirty-nine. Though her mother tried her best to ignore this bad timing and not blame Lilly for it, she was never very successful.

Three years went by with Kay struggling to keep up with Charlotte's talent and missing out on Lilly in the meanwhile. It was always, "Come along, Lilly. Don't hold us up, dear. Charlotte can't be late." Lilly would hop on one foot and twirl around in an ungainly fashion. Kay Darling was so focused on Charlotte that she hadn't noticed the twisted femur. What with being a young widow and having such a talented first-born, she didn't have time to zero in on the various imperfections of her second-born.

Lilly was a child easily lost in her own thoughts, and as she was chasing after autumn leaves, she was thinking about *Peter Pan.* Eight-year-old

Charlotte was playing that role in the lower school play, and Lilly was going to be one of the Darling children. She figured the play was written about them. Darling was the family name, after all. But where was Nana, the dog? Lilly was lonely and wanted Nana, but a dog wouldn't promote Charlotte in any way. There would never be a dog for Lilly, and she knew it.

Kay and Lilly's worlds revolved around Charlotte. There was never enough to be done for her. Lilly knew this, but it was like knowing the sky is blue, an impersonal fact, not to be questioned or resented. Charlotte knew her mother and sister's lives revolved around her, and for her, like for Lilly, it was an impersonal fact, nothing to be proud of or to feel guilty about.

This rehearsal would have been like all the others, except there were costumes. Charlotte was conspicuously graceful and glided around in a green leotard, while Lilly sat quietly in a white Victorian nightgown. She had been told how lucky she was to be in the big-girl play, but she didn't believe it. If she were not sitting in the corner with a big blue bow in her mouse brown hair, maybe she could be at the stables with Nina.

Lilly always remembered to bring sugar cubes for Cocoa. She had to reach up to stroke his neck, laughing when his muzzle caressed her back. Sometimes Charlotte would let Lilly sit on him, secretly hoping to turn the pony over to her little sister. She wanted to perform, not ride, but it would be hard to give Cocoa away, since the pony had been a gift from her father.

Most of all, Charlotte made every effort to hang on to memories of her father, but he was fading fast. Every night, after her pretty young mother had heard her prayers and tucked her in, they would talk about how much Roy stilled loved them. Then Charlotte would visualize him in as much detail as possible. It frightened her that he was becoming less and less real to her.

Charlotte had been named in her father's will, but he hadn't had time to name Lilly, and the will was not written with provisions for future progeny. Kay always meant to make this up to Lilly, but she never did, as she needed every dime and more to give Charlotte the advantages her natural talent demanded. She never considered what Lilly's natural talents might have been. There was no time for such considerations. Rushing from event to event with Charlotte took all of her. And anyway, Lilly was a clumsy little thing with not much to say. She certainly didn't need to attend the Washington School of Ballet three times a week or have private lessons every Saturday.

Eventually, Kay would suggest Charlotte give Cocoa to Nina's riding school. That horse was eating money needed for singing lessons. The children's choir at the Upperville church was not demanding enough for someone of Charlotte's caliber. Kay would have to look further afield and further afield always meant further financial and energy expenditures.

Kay's mission was to make Charlotte ready for destiny when it called. She could be a classical ballerina, a Broadway idol or on the silver screen. All of this was possible, and Kay would do her part to make things happen. Charlotte Darling would not fail to be a star.

The three performances of Peter Pan were well attended by parents and friends as well as the whole student body, and it was Charlotte's first taste of fame. She found it delicious. Outrageously delicious, like the shiny red candied apples made especially for the cast. The combination was exhilarating.

Kay allowed Charlotte to wear the Peter Pan costume to riding class with the substitution of a hard hat for the feathered felt one. Nina wasn't so sure this clinging to the role after the play was over was good for Charlotte and wanted to mention this to Kay at the end of the Sunday afternoon session. Instead, she was surprised by Charlotte coming up to her.

"Miss Nina, Cocoa told me he wants more out of life than just waiting around for me. I want to give him to your school so lots of kids can ride him."

"Charlotte, this is a big decision. Does your mother know?"

"She says I'll need to spend more and more time singing and dancing now that I'm eight. She said I won't have much time for riding anymore and that Dad would understand."

Kay was inside the stable, reading in the little anteroom provided for waiting parents, but Lilly, who was standing next to Nina, started to cry.

Nina squatted down and put an arm around both girls and held them close. "You girls are always welcome, and Cocoa will be right here waiting for you. And when you're ready, Lilly, you can join the beginner class."

"I'm ready, Miss Nina. And I know how to get here. If Mom's too busy to bring me, I can walk."

Nina could feel the back of her throat tighten.

Kay and Nina agreed. Cocoa now belonged to Nina, and both Lilly and Charlotte were invited to all appropriate classes at no charge. Nina told Kay one of the other instructors could pick Lilly up, if that would be of help.

"Oh, yes," said Kay, "That would be a big help." And from that September day for as long as they were in Middleburg, Lilly stopped being an appendage at Charlotte's lessons and started becoming a frequent fixture at Nina's riding school.

In December, Charlotte danced the part of a snowflake in the Washington Ballet's *Nutcracker*. During the first rehearsal, the ballet mistress, Natasha Jitkoff, found Charlotte in tears outside the green room. She bent down to the level of the little girl.

"What could make such a beautiful snowflake cry?"

"It's the music. I feel it pouring over me like honey, and I want to get inside it. But I can't find the door."

Starting in January, Natasha took Charlotte on as her personal protégé and reported Charlotte's words about the music verbatim to the Washington Post. When Kay read the article on *The Nutcracker Suite* with Charlotte's quote, she knew the die was cast, and all her energy from then on went into making Charlotte the world's most famous dancer.

Charlotte thought back on this period of her life and typed.

> "Despite my father's untimely death, I had a truly idyllic childhood in the Virginia countryside. Lots of dogs and horses and, by age nine, the constant

and undivided attention of the incomparable Natasha. She taught me how to slip inside the music and dance from where the golden sweetness is. She taught me how to protect myself from harmful vibrations and bask in healing ones, how to soar towards the light and linger there. Music makes me whole. I can feel it in the marrow of my ballet-dancing bones."

CHAPTER THREE

"Come in, Priscilla dear," Charlotte called from her bed. Priscilla was her PA, an attractive, efficient mid-thirties redhead who knew how to deal with Charlotte. The luncheon tray on the bed held the remains of a club sandwich and a rectangular dark green box. "These After Eights don't taste right, and they definitely aren't thin enough."

"Mrs. Darling, we've been through this before. They've been this way for twenty-five years, and there's nothing more like the originals than these."

"Then email that place in London and order their mints. Bendick's. And get some of those violet creams from that other place. Have them overnighted."

"Okay." Priscilla made the word sound like it came from a cheerleader. "They'll arrive on Monday."

"Isn't it funny that London has all the best chocolates? It's supposed to be Switzerland or Belgium or someplace, but nooooo. Now it's London where they all hide out."

Priscilla nodded philosophically and waited.

"And don't be stingy. Get big boxes."

"I'll get right on it, Mrs. D."

"And don't roll your eyes, Priscilla. These are quality sweets. I bet both shops have royal warrants."

For nearly twelve years, Priscilla had worked for Charlotte. She had all the right addresses and knew all the fine points. Like, get Mallomars, not

Pinwheels. Make sure chocolate chip cookies are crisp and brownies soft. Always have Cheetos and M&Ms in stock. Make sure photographers know Charlotte's light must come from the left at a forty-five degree angle. Be sure her Coke comes in glass bottles and is made with sugar cane, not corn syrup. One of Charlotte's favorite rants concerned Coca-Cola and its ever-changing formulas. Charlotte only wanted what she called 'regular' Coke, and she needed several a week. She felt it was an inalienable right to have the Coke of her childhood, and vociferously regretted the heroics involved in procuring it, while failing to mention the heroics were never performed by her. Her staff had to find Coke with a yellow cap.

Priscilla was always surprised at how many fans wanted to know what kind of diet Charlotte followed. She had to equivocate and pass them on to PR, who definitely didn't want to go public with the facts. Everyone, even Charlotte, agreed it was frightful for one of the greatest American dancers of all time to be a junk foodie, but she liked what she liked, and that was that. PR wanted her to be perceived as a crystal-clean vegan, if possible, or at the very least, a lacto-vegetarian. The smoking kept them pulling their hair.

Charlotte was cooperative, though, and never smoked in public. She scrupulously forced herself to eat what she called 'penance meals' in front of journalists and went along with whatever idea Priscilla had for hiding her obsession. But now with everyone being a photographer, this was becoming problematic. She told PR she would drink regular Cokes wherever she could get them but agreed to eat Cheetos only at home, to thoroughly wash the orange color off after indulging in them and let Priscilla be the one to buy the Devil Dogs at the deli.

Never forgetting that her heroine, Margot Fonteyn, was the consummate professional, Charlotte was always gracious as well as graceful, always on time and exquisitely polite. She had assumed this role very young and only her family and staff ever glimpsed another Charlotte. And that was only occasionally. She had fewer meltdowns than most stars, but they did happen.

Charlotte truly appreciated PR. She knew they were right. But she was a rebel, and today she was rebelling against Margot, who'd been dead for decades.

Early that evening while stretching at the ballet barre in her bedroom, Charlotte put the phone on speaker and pressed Lilly's name.

Lilly could hear the highly polished mahogany barre whispering in the background before her sister started speaking. She was not expecting an apology for the earlier hang up, nor did she think Charlotte would require one from her. Charlotte got cranky sometimes. Lilly vaguely wondered if it wasn't so much menopause and had more to do with the pills.

"I'm mad at Margot." Charlotte's husky voice was slightly breathless.

Lilly closed her computer, glanced at her reflection in the windowpane across from her desk and sat up straight. She was alert. Being mad at Margot was something unheard of. She put the phone on speaker, slid on her glasses and picked up her embroidery hoop. From a lifetime of waiting and listening, Lilly had become an embroiderer par excellence. She could hear and think better with her hands occupied.

"Mad at Margot?" Lilly had learned to master her voice, too. She set the program on neutral.

"You know she didn't even meet Nureyev until she was forty-two. Her greatest dancing was done at an age when all sensible dancers have long since retired. And I'm fifty-three."

"Where's this going?" Lilly twisted the scarlet silk and held the needle up to the light.

"Tandem has someone interested in making my memoir into a film. With me dancing. And I don't have a Rudolf up my sleeve to inspire and squire me."

"Hmm."

"Everyone expects me to exceed her. But how can I ever even measure up?"

Lilly put her hoop down and frowned. This was a totally new concept. "You've always measured up. And it was your idea to compete with Margot, anyway." Voice still set on neutral.

"I'm tired, Lilly. And to keep up with her, I'd have to continue dancing for another seven years and then appear in special roles for another seven years after that. That's fourteen."

"I can do the math."

"Lilly, don't you see? I just can't." Lilly could hear the barre creaking. Energetic, rhythmic stretching was going on, although there was a definite tightness in Charlotte's voice.

"Of course you can, dear." Lilly switched the setting to soothe.

"No, I can't. I need you. There's a strange sort of loneliness stalking me, deep and black and wide. It's gotten worse and worse over the past few weeks. I feel breathless. Can you come over, please? I don't think I can shake this alone."

"On my way." Back to neutral, but Lilly moved quickly. She swept the embroidery silks into a special bag and made sure the excellent scissors shaped like the Eiffel Tower and the horn-rimmed glasses were safe in their cases before shrugging on her camouflage jacket to take the two block walk westward to Park Avenue. It was late October. Night was falling fast, and the brilliant yellow leaves wafting down from the gingko trees were loud, complaining of brittleness. A brisk breeze chased them along the sidewalk heading towards Central Park.

Lilly's face was drawn as she hurried towards the magnificent limestone building at 740 Park Avenue. Charlotte had never made a cry for help like this before. Many cries were made for help dressing or planning or babysitting, but never before a cry from the heart. She was worried about Charlotte and wondered what percentage of her life had been spent like this. She didn't put a number on it but imagined it would be too high to contemplate with equanimity. She used the entrance on 71st Street. Charlotte lived in the 'D' line.

"'Evening, Joe," Lilly said to the doorman.

"'Evening, Miss Darling. Mr. Buatta is up there with Mrs. D."

Lilly had to hand it to Charlotte. Everybody loved her. She always made sure there were tickets available for the doormen to take their families to dress rehearsals at Lincoln Center, and she took good care of them at Christmas. She knew the amount of entertaining she had to do meant more work for them. She always greeted each one personally, often asking about children or aged parents by name.

Charlotte lived at the very top of the 'D' line in a perfectly proportioned fourteen room apartment. Mario Buatta had decorated it twenty years before with the magic wand of timeless beauty that covered him with so much fame. He was a tall good-looking man who knew how to dress, and Lilly loved his sense of humor. She counted herself lucky that he'd dropped in.

She pressed sixteen on the elevator panel so as to enter the duplex on the lower floor. Charlotte rarely locked the door to her apartment, and Lilly walked into the spacious sky blue entrance hall. She tilted her head and could hear the famous decorator's laugh. Over the years Mario had become the family favorite and was welcome with or without an invitation anytime. She could hear him teasing Charlotte and Charlotte responding in kind.

Lilly let up on the adrenalin pedal a bit and walked past the curving marble staircase. She stood at the door of the red lacquered library for thirty seconds or so before Charlotte noticed her. "Lilly! Come in. Look who's here! Please join us for supper." Lilly got a whiff of the clean floral scent of Prima. Charlotte stood before her encased in a green silk caftan with her hair neatly bound at the nape of her neck, having transformed herself in a matter of minutes from an emotional wreck to a glamorous goddess of dance. Only a lifetime on stage prepared a person to accomplish a feat like that.

"Please stay, Lilly," Mario pleaded. "I need protection. Your sister's driving me crazy. Do I look tired? See these circles under my eyes? They weren't there when I arrived here five minutes ago. All this toe pointing and arabesque-ing is wearing me out."

"Good to see you, Mario." Lilly gave him a cursory kiss on the cheek and looked past him, out of the window and onto the Midtown Manhattan lights, playing for time. Did she want to stay? Mario was fun and could get her out of herself. And what else did she have to do?

"I'd love to have dinner with you two."

"Then be an angel and go tell Gani we'll be three and that we could use some hors d'oeuvres in here." A couple from the Philippines worked for Charlotte and made sure that she never had to know what happened in the kitchen.

"Where's Colin?" Lilly asked.

"Who knows? He said he was going to London to visit his mother, but he could be anywhere. This is what I love about the twenty-first century. I don't have to know." Charlotte had seen what had gone into Colin's suitcase and was reasonably sure London wasn't on the itinerary.

Charlotte was her public persona all evening and didn't ask Lilly to stay or mention the phone call when saying goodnight to Lilly and Mario at nine-thirty.

Half an hour later, Lilly answered her phone.

"I don't know what got into me, Lil. Forget about what I said earlier."

"You had me worried. When did Colin leave?"

"This afternoon. You know, I watched him walk back and forth through the bedroom while he was packing, and I have to admit, he's still a great looking man. He has that lean athletic look I love. Not all pumped up from weightlifting like dancers. Imagine, despite everything, I still lust after him, through all these years."

"No regrets, then?"

"I have plenty of regrets, as you very well know. Just not on the physical front."

"Well, that's something."

"What's weird for this day and age is that he's the only man I've ever been with."

"Your body was a professional asset from a very early age. You couldn't have left it lying around in any old bed."

"What about you, Lilly? Has yours been lying around any beds lately?"

Lilly laughed and said goodnight.

Charlotte actually had no idea what her sister's sex life was like. She'd never raised the subject, nor had she ever told anyone, even Lilly, that sex frightened and repulsed her. She was deeply ashamed of this.

CHAPTER FOUR

At six the next morning Charlotte began her rigorous routine. She took a great deal of pleasure in this ritual, and afterwards, as she showered and washed her hair, she thought about Chuck Elliot. He had been her boyfriend in the seventh grade. They'd held hands all through the fall, and on New Year's Day, as they sat side by side listening to music on a plump chintz sofa in the living room of the fieldstone farmhouse, his face came towards her. She held her breath but forgot to close her eyes, and all she could see as he came closer and closer was a spray of ripe pimples blooming on his eighth grade cheek. She turned her head just in time. They were shy of each other after that and only said, "Hi," in the halls as they passed on the way to class. But the incident triggered some distant memory, vague but menacing. Not something she wanted to woo into clarity.

Six months after this almost-kiss, Kay sold the house in Middleburg and moved her young family to an apartment in Washington. The driving had become too much for her, and she thought Charlotte needed to be in a major city. The girls were enrolled in the National Cathedral School and neither went to school with a boy ever again. Weekends in Middleburg were still on for Lilly, thanks to Nina, but by that time, Charlotte's serious lifework had begun, and for her, Middleburg was only possible on special occasions.

Suddenly, Charlotte was twenty-one and had never been kissed. Of course, she'd read sex books and heard her schoolmates talking and talking of nothing else. She'd leered and laughed but found the whole thing revolting.

Charlotte shook her head as if to rearrange her memories and opened the Word document. She propped herself up on the mountain of pillows and stared at the screen, thinking of her husband.

Colin Stone arrived in Washington at age eighteen with the intention of spending a year touring the States, surviving on a small savings and a talent for shooting pool. His student visa allowed him to work part-time, and his first job was moving stage sets at the Kennedy Center. Charlotte, prompt as always for rehearsal, first heard his voice coming from behind her. It was his delectable British accent that first caught her attention, but it was his blond, green-eyed good looks and tall, lanky body that held it.

Charlotte sat in front of her computer, wanting to record all these memories, but for some reason the words weren't coming. Never having been one to observe Sabbath rest, Charlotte picked up the phone and called her sister. "I want to write about meeting Colin today, while he's out of town. Will you come over and help me remember?"

"Write it any way you want. That's the beauty of a memoir."

"You can be such a pain in the ass sometimes, Lil. Just come for lunch, and we'll get the photograph albums out afterwards. And maybe call Mom."

Knowing she had to go didn't make it easier. Lilly had watched her mother manage Charlotte's career from the beginning. She'd learned from a master and was the natural successor in this demanding, but highly remunerative role. She was now well off in her own right, and with Colin's having made such a mess of things, she'd found herself the one with the cash. Her salary was a percentage of Charlotte's gross income, which meant she'd profited from many years of success, and with a banker, rather than a husband, making financial decisions, she was protected from owning things like second-rate retina scanners. Lilly liked to watch her money grow, and although she never spent much on her apartment, she did buy one classic Valentino item each fall and each spring. And shoes. She was a sucker for shoes.

Grudgingly, Lilly agreed with the voice in her head, which reminded her if it had not been for Charlotte's amazing talent, she would not have had a life filled with luxury world-travel nor would she own a splendid co-op on the Upper East Side of Manhattan. She'd probably be working with horses as a riding teacher or exerciser or something like that. Maybe even running Nina's place. That would have been a nice life, maybe a better life, and she allowed herself to long for it another moment before she pulled on her clothes and headed over to Charlotte's.

During the short walk over to Park Avenue, she let her mind wander back and forth from Middleburg to New York. By the time she arrived, she knew she was content with her lot in life. She was where she wanted to be. It was fine she'd never married. She liked working for her famous sister and was devoted to her niece. She appreciated the travel and interesting people she met with Charlotte.

When Lilly arrived, Charlotte was rested and dressed in Prada jeans and a pale blue cashmere sweater. She had on metallic cobalt leather flats—the Italian ones whose designer had photos of her on his ads running in all the high-end fashion magazines. Her lips and right hand were bright orange from Cheetos. Five large leather photograph albums were stacked on the lacquered linen coffee table. Charlotte was seated in the center of a curved sofa that rounded off a corner of the library in front of a window.

"God, I can't get over the weight of these things. Sit next to me and prepare to laugh out loud."

Lilly sat and bent over the album open on Charlotte's lap.

"Here I am as Peter Pan. And look at you, little Miss Darling." Charlotte pointed at a faded snapshot on the lower left.

Lilly felt a rush of compassion for her own sad little face that peered out at the camera from under a big satin bow in the corner of the photograph of Charlotte. "I thought we were going to remember meeting Colin today."

"All in due time, my dear," Charlotte said in her older and wiser sister voice. "I asked a few people for lunch. They'll be here soon, and I have to wash off the lethal orange."

Six people showed up for lunch. Charlotte was cheerful and charming, but it was late afternoon by the time the last guest left. They never got around to remembering meeting Colin or calling Mom.

Accustomed as she was to Charlotte's need to be distracted when not on stage, Lilly was not even slightly annoyed that the impromptu luncheon had changed the plan. Lilly had become so flexible from fitting into

Charlotte's wishes since early childhood, that she barely registered deviations from one idea to the next.

The next day Pricilla came into the library at ten-thirty to find Charlotte quietly working at her computer, demurely dressed for the day, which included luncheon with Lilly, two PR people, as well as an interviewer and a photographer from *Vain Fare* magazine.

"Priscilla, please, please tell me you can find some Russell Stover marshmallow turkeys. Maybe they have them in New Jersey. You can't believe what Gani has planned for lunch."

"You know they don't have those turkeys until November." Priscilla pressed her lips together.

"What about some Peeps? They have all kinds of Peeps available all year round now. Please. For lunch it's vegetable broth with gluten-free vermicelli, followed by kale and quinoa salad garnished with squash blossoms topped off with pomegranate sorbet made with wild honey and an oatcake. I ask you, how do these things happen to me? If I could have something delicious before they get here and something to look forward to afterwards, I can make it."

"If this is an emergency, I happen to have some M&Ms Peanuts in my office."

"Don't be so sure. I invaded your supply over the weekend. Please get me something marshmallow-y right away and without the eye-roll, if possible, sweetie."

"I know you're mad that I saw your blood report, but you're the one who left it on the hall table. Your triglycerides are off the charts. I'm sure Dr. Ellis talks to you about the dangers of this."

"He does. He talks and talks about it until we're both bright blue in the face. Some people need more sugar than others. My interview starts at eleven-thirty. Get what you can and hurry back."

"This could lead to diabetes. I wish you wouldn't be so careless about your health."

"I need the sugar. Look at all the energy I expend. Stop mother-hen-ing me and get going."

The guests had arrived by the time Priscilla returned with the goods. She could tell from the entrance hall that the interview was going well and didn't want to interrupt. Two hours later, as coffee was being served in the living room, Charlotte called Priscilla in, introduced her and invited her to join them.

The very thin and severely dressed interviewer turned to Priscilla and said, "Mrs. Darling is amazing. I saw she didn't even *touch* her oatcake. And drank only green tea. Awesomely pure. You're so lucky to work here."

"Mrs. Darling is a lot of fun to work for."

"I love your top."

"Claudie Pierlot. A present from Mrs. Darling."

"She's so fabulous, and guess what, she's officially agreed to contribute some of her favorite recipes for *Menus from the Thin and Famous*, our first cookbook, which comes out next year," he said.

"Oh, that'll be super interesting." Priscilla concentrated on making eye contact.

"We'll want some pictures of her in her kitchen. I'll call you to make arrangements. Hope she'll include today's delicious lunch."

"She'd be delighted for sure. This is one of her favorite luncheon menus."

Priscilla could tell Charlotte was getting uncomfortable. From the corner of her eye, she saw Charlotte trying to get her attention. She knew from long experience, Charlotte was ready for some peace and sugar.

"I hate to spoil this lovely gathering, but I need Mrs. Darling for another appointment in a few minutes." Priscilla helped see the guests out.

Charlotte didn't let Lilly go, but the others left, each one thinking Charlotte understood, appreciated and cherished them. She had the gift of making others feel special, and she was generous with it.

"Priscilla, bring whatever you've procured to the library right away." Charlotte steered her sister into the red room. "Lilly, let's get the albums out. Can you believe how long it's been since I met Colin?"

"I was sixteen and can still remember how crazy you were about him. The whole thing was so romantic." Lilly looked closely at the dates on the leather spines of the albums precisely lined up on carefully arranged shelves and pulled out a thick navy blue volume. She handed it to Charlotte and sat next to her on the sofa.

"It was romantic, wasn't it? You and I had lived such sheltered lives, and then came Colin with his wry humor and quick wit. So handsome and full of energy. Not to mention his irresistible accent." Charlotte opened the album on her lap.

"He brought a lot of laughter to the three of us. Mom always says he reminds her of Dad." Lilly had a far-off look in her eye.

"Mom only sees what she wants to see. And it was great for a while. Anyway, I want to write about it in the best light. I'm mad as hell now, but we'll get through this. I can't imagine ever getting divorced."

"I can't imagine continuing to live with someone who'd put me in financial peril."

"He didn't do it on purpose, and anyway, even when he's here, we don't see each other much. He's been sleeping in his study for ages." Charlotte thought the actual amount of those ages would shock Lilly. Nearly twenty years. Twenty years of touching only in front of people and kissing only for the camera.

"Thanks for doing this with me, Lil. Sometimes it's scary to walk around in the past alone."

"Don't say that. You've led a charmed life."

"Here comes Priscilla, thank God. What have you got in that bag?"

"Charleston Chews, Russell Stover Mint Dreams—sorry, no turkeys yet—and a box of Mallomars. Couldn't find any Peeps. This is the best I could do, in the marshmallow vein." Priscilla looked into the bag. "Oh, and a bag of actual marshmallows, for toasting over the fire, if you feel so inclined."

"Just leave everything here. How long before we can expect those deliveries from London?"

"Later this afternoon."

"Bring them right on in when they come. Lilly and I will be here doing research for the book."

"Shall I hold the calls?"

"Only the boring ones."

Lilly left just as the boxes arrived from London. Charlotte and Priscilla sampled the contents and agreed, they were, indeed, quality sweets worthy of their royal warrants. Charlotte sprayed her all-time favorite perfume, '1000' by Jean Patou, all over herself to help her remember the beginning of the love affair with Colin. Preferring prosaic fare, however, she opened a small bag of Cheetos to encourage herself while she wrote.

> "Thirty-two years ago, I stood center-stage at the Kennedy Center waiting for the curtain to rise on my love life, and suddenly it swooshed up with lightning speed. Colin walked onto that very stage, and it was love at first sight. I was twenty-one, Colin eighteen. When I heard his baritone voice and saw his handsome face, my brain chemistry changed for good and ever. With Colin and our precious Topsy, I live an enchanted life full of love and romance, music and flowers."

Charlotte raised her eyes from the computer screen and narrowed them. She considered who might suspect this wasn't entirely accurate. Well, let's see, she thought. There's Colin, of course, and Topsy. Lilly. Priscilla and probably PR. And Mom and Nina. I'm safe. None of them would want it otherwise.

"Oh, shut up, Lilly," was her recurrent thought as she whipped out two thousand words on Word.

CHAPTER FIVE

Kay Darling and Nina Pipes arrived in New York on Tuesday before Thanksgiving. The guest room beds were made up with green and white Porthault sheets and included two large and a small pillow on each bed. Though it was pretty, Kay privately thought Charlotte was too extravagant, and as yet, she didn't know the full extent of the financial losses. She didn't mention her qualms to Nina who would only tell her it was Charlotte's money and she'd worked hard for it. Nina would be right, of course, and Kay held her tongue.

Nina was thrilled to be in New York. She loved this guest room with the green and white toile de Jouy curtains and wall covering for both the room and bath. She plopped herself down on her twin bed and surveyed the perfection of the large space. "Kay, I can hear you thinking. What's going on in that head of yours?"

"I was thinking we should take a walk and pick up some of those chocolate covered marshmallow turkeys that Charlotte likes and some lilies for Lilly."

"Great idea. You go do that, and I'm going to finish my book. I feel so contented just being in this room. I don't want to leave it." Whatever Nina said sounded wonderful. She had a bell-like quality to her voice, and Kay hesitated a moment, wanting to let her have her way, leaving her to curl up with her book.

"Oh, for God's sake, Nina. Get your ass in gear."

Nina had suffered a mild stroke eight months previously, and Kay wanted to keep an eye on her. It had been the doctor's recommendation for her to walk an hour everyday. Nina, who'd spent her life on the back of a horse, and Kay, who'd spent her life at dance rehearsals, had suddenly changed places.

Nina heaved a theatrical sigh, "Okay. You win. Let's get the walk over with."

It had been lonely for Kay after Lilly took over managing Charlotte, and nine years ago, she'd accepted Nina's invitation and moved into Covert, Nina's family place in Middleburg. Nina had been rattling around by herself and was happy for the company. Together the two women let their hair turn gray. Nina's was steel colored and closely cropped, which was a suitable topping for her lean, muscular frame. Kay became zaftig, and her white hair was soft and fine. One day without warning she colored her hair a honey blond. She thought the dye gave her hair some body and was secretly pleased that it made her look years younger than Nina.

For all that time, Nina had prodded Kay every day to ride or walk or do anything at all other than sit in front of the Turner Classic channel. Now it was Kay who was prodding Nina.

They walked forty blocks and all the stores were out of turkeys, and Nina suggested buying Santas. Kay nixed this, "She doesn't like Santas. Only turkeys. And I'm sure she's the sole reason there're none to be had on the Upper East Side."

"I would have thought she'd have grown out of chocolate covered marshmallow things by now."

"Maybe next year." Kay gave Nina a sidelong glance.

It was just the family that night at Lilly's for dinner. Lilly, Kay, Nina, Topsy, Charlotte and Colin, who said, "All my favorite ladies at once. No one has it better than me! I'm the luckiest man in New York."

"Colin can be counted on for charm and flattery." Charlotte's voice had a touch of bitterness in it, and Kay looked up in alarm. No one else seemed to notice, and the evening passed without a hitch. Kay and Nina were easy.

Kay had had to become easy, but nine years of retirement in Middleburg had buffed off most of her stage-mother edges.

Nina had rightfully claimed a position in the Darling family. She was the cool head to go to in crisis, the shoulder to cry on and the pocket to pick, especially in the early days when things were tight. She was cherished by one and all.

When Charlotte said she was not financing another semester, Topsy had first gone to Kay, but Kay wanted to know what she was planning on doing once she had her PhD in English Lit. Topsy was vague saying something about teaching and writing. Kay passed on financing her. She'd always been disappointed in Topsy and thought her untalented and self-absorbed. She didn't mention this to Nina as Nina would remind her Topsy was a beauty as well as being all there was in the way of a new generation for the family. Kay sometimes hated that Nina was always right.

Moving on from Kay to Nina, Topsy found an easy touch. "This is just between you and me. When I die my estate will be split between you and Lilly. But if I die first, your grandmother will have the right to live out her life at Covert. So if I give you a 'loan' now, you won't have to repay me. I'll arrange this so that it's equitable in the end. My end, that is." Topsy, at least, had the grace to be embarrassed by this and didn't mention to any of the others that Nina was funding her. She told them she'd gotten a student loan, but the thing was that the lie made her uncomfortable. Uncomfortable particularly around Kay and Nina. Kay noticed this, too.

That night, in the green and white room, once they were settled and the lights were out, Kay said, "Did you notice anything strange between Charlotte and Colin?"

"No. They were overly affectionate, as usual. Why?" Nina was tired and wanted to go to sleep.

"I felt Charlotte wasn't herself. Colin kept checking his phone, and what's gotten into Topsy? That girl's something. Totally self-satisfied and opinionated." Kay knew it was unnatural not to be enamored of her granddaughter, but she wasn't, and she would be honest with herself on that score.

"Now, Kay, admit it, you would only be happy with another star to launch. Talent like Charlotte's doesn't materialize in every generation, you know."

"Topsy's lazy and spoiled. She'd have halted Charlotte's career more than once, if I hadn't been there to set things straight."

"Poor old Topsy. You were always focused on Charlotte; Charlotte always focused on dance, and Colin only focused on money, so who was there to focus on Topsy?"

"Lilly and you. And Topsy herself, that's who. All three of you focusing only on Topsy, especially Topsy focusing on Topsy. And it shows. I keep hoping she'll grow out of it, but she's already twenty-seven."

"Hush, now and go to sleep. You don't really feel that way."

Kay said goodnight politely, but she didn't go to sleep, and she really did feel that way. She replayed the evening in her mind and wondered what was going on that she wasn't privy to. She was still the lioness protecting Charlotte. It had been her life's work. What was bothering her girl? It could be money or Colin or menopause or maybe she was burned out. She was fifty-three after all. But no, it wasn't that. Kay was sure it wasn't that. Could it be something she didn't even suspect?

Thanksgiving dinner would be at Charlotte's. Her dining room was painted with a dozen layers of paint. Mario had brought a ripe cantaloupe and opened it up in front of Hans, his most talented painter, and said, "Make the walls exactly like this, juicy and intense. For the ceiling use shades of the same blue as the hall and put some fluffy clouds up there for Mrs. Darling and a long silver lightning bolt." Once the cantaloupe color sample was set, Mario had silk dyed to match for the curtains. Then an Oushak carpet was specially woven. It was undoubtedly the prettiest dining room in New York.

Ten years later, Charlotte was dancing at La Fenice in Venice and between performances, Lilly lured her to a convent where the nuns did the most meticulous embroidery. Together they designed four tablecloths for that room. They ordered unusually large napkins without embroidery. Lilly would do those herself. Every Thanksgiving ever since, they'd used the heavy linen cloth that was the same color as the walls. Embroidered fall leaves in all their glorious colors were lavishly scattered across it, bright yellow, shocking pinky red, rust, crimson and gold. Each napkin had a different color leaf.

This year, Charlotte put gold candles in the silver candelabras and arranged mimosas in the five centerpieces marching down the long table. Normally, she didn't like out of season flowers, but when she saw them in the window of Ronaldo Maia's shop, she couldn't resist their ephemeral beauty and gave in. She'd make an exception this year. The other exceptions she'd make would be to eat as much as she wanted of everything, no matter who was watching, drink regular Coke throughout the meal and not share the marshmallow turkeys.

As it turned out, the evening was a triumph of deliciousness. Eighteen people beautifully dressed, interesting conversations, Gani's traditional Thanksgiving dinner, and a strolling violinist. Charlotte was relaxed and gracious, Colin the perfect host, Topsy at her smiling best.

Later in the guest room Kay whispered to Nina, "Why on earth would Colin be checking his phone constantly on Thanksgiving?"

"Colin is always checking his phone. He may have a deal cooking somewhere."

"It's too late for that somewhere to be Europe, and he never cooks in Asia."

"Maybe he's started." Nina yawned and switched off the bedside lamp.

A few days later, Kay made a point of having lunch alone with Colin. They met at Café Americano right around the corner on Lexington and 70th.

"How's my favorite son-in-law?"

Colin started his defense right away, "You know, Kay, this decision I made with the optics company could turn around and make a lot of money. But

Charlotte has demonized me and jumped to the worst-case scenario. The last six months have been hell. I know it's her money, but cancelling the lease on my office was a low blow."

"I'm so sorry, darling. Charlotte has an artist's temperament and having that temperament has put her where she is, so we cannot expect her to be otherwise."

"It's very hard to live with that day in and day out."

Kay stiffened. "I think you need to consider what you just said. Marriage *is* day in and day out. Life's not easy for anyone, and thanks to Charlotte, your life has been about as easy as it gets."

Colin looked as if his breath had been knocked out of him. Decades of complacency were shattered with those few words, but his defense redoubled. "I might make it look easy, Kay, but Charlotte can be difficult."

"Don't think any of this is easy for Charlotte. The demands of a dance career are extreme, and she's never slacked a day in her life."

"You don't understand. She's only focused on her career and rarely has time for Topsy and me. We're always available to her, but she's never available to us. Even when she's not performing, she spends the day at the studio."

"Of course, when she's not performing, she has to be rehearsing. That's how it works, Colin. Now, let's drop this and order our lunch."

Kay was silent on the flight from LaGuardia to Dulles, and just as the plane was about to land, she came alive. "Nina, Colin's up to no good. I absolutely know it."

"Kay, stop it. He's been a perfectly good son-in-law for thirty-two years. Why would you say such a thing?"

"I've spent fifty-three years watching how life affects Charlotte, and something is threatening her. And it's Colin. He's acting guilty. I don't think she gets it, whatever 'it' is. She thinks it's all a bad business deal and another affair, but there's more. I'm sure of it."

In the car going back to Middleburg, Kay's mind churned. She would protect her daughter no matter what.

CHAPTER SIX

The Nutcracker Suite Family Benefit was on December 10th, and Charlotte made sure the doormen with children had the best seats. She invited them backstage to drink hot chocolate and went with them to the party, introducing them to some Candy Canes and Dewdrops and many Snowflakes.

Charlotte had danced the Sugar Plum Fairy role for decades but never ceased to be exhilarated by it. It was strenuous, though, and December had to be dedicated only to dance. Priscilla was in charge of presents, Gani in charge of feasts, and Ronaldo Maia was in charge of trees, garlands, mistletoe and flowers.

This kind of organization left Colin and Topsy without any duties. Topsy hung out with her friends and sulked in her apartment on Gramercy Park, and once more Kay was right, Colin spent his time with his current inamorata, Jasmine, in her apartment on Central Park West.

Jasmine was born in China, and her real name was Fang, meaning 'fragrant' in Chinese. When at age five, she moved to New York City with her parents, her naturalized American aunt suggested that Fang's name be changed to Jasmine. That was twenty years ago, and still, there were many who would say her original name suited her perfectly and should never have been changed.

Colin rang her doorbell while unbuckling his belt.

She started right in. "Colin, how could you let that rotten old sugar plum take your office away? What's the matter with you? Don't you like to fuck me with a view of Madison Avenue anymore? By the way, I don't like you sniffing around my place day and night, like you do. Neighbors talk."

Colin pulled his pants down around his ankles and sat on an armless chair. "Jasmine, calm down. And take off your clothes." Jasmine did as she was told, but only because she wanted to. She loved the way Colin used her. She was wet before her lace panties hit the floor.

"Come sit on my cock, like a good girl." She spread her legs over his lap and took his penis inside her. They stayed completely still, tense and panting, for as long as they possibly could, then erupted in frantic movement. Colin had been rough with her nipples, the bruises were vivid, but she wanted him to make them hurt. That's the way they both liked it. Once they were spent, the bickering began again and lasted well into the night. And so it went day after day, starting at around four in the afternoon. The Christmas tree blinked in the background.

Kay and Nina arrived in New York on Christmas Eve. Charlotte had performances that day at one and again at five, but after that she was free until the two o'clock matinee on the 26th. Charlotte's rigorous schedule was no surprise, and the two women had traditionally spent the week between Christmas and New Year's with Colin and Topsy. This year, it became apparent that they would be on their own.

This was no hardship to them as Kay and Nina both enjoyed museums and energetically whisked themselves from one to the other, with one afternoon dedicated to *The Nutcracker*. When at the apartment, however, Kay stationed herself in the library and observed Colin's every movement.

For Christmas dinner another of the Venetian tablecloths graced the table. This one was dark green with gold stars of various sizes glittering on it. Lilly did a spectacular job on the napkins but swore it was the last time she would use metallic thread.

The turkey was laden with truffles, and dessert was the steamed raspberry pudding, which had been the finale of Christmas dinner for as long as anyone could remember. It was Kay's grandmother's recipe. And Charlotte had one of her friends from the Metropolitan Opera Company come dressed as Santa and sing Christmas carols between courses. Everyone joined in the singing, and later, they said, "No one does Christmas like Charlotte." Lilly could not help but think, "No one does Christmas like Priscilla, Gani, Ronaldo and the singing Santa."

By January 1st, Kay, the amateur sleuth, decided she needed to seek the help of a professional. She told Nina she felt Charlotte was in some kind of danger. Nina told her she was nuts and not to meddle. But before going back to Middleburg, Kay hired a private detective called Jack Harding.

During the drive from Dulles airport to Middleburg, Kay said, "I feel much better now that Mr. Harding will find out what Colin's up to. This is not like one of his usual affairs. This time he feels guilty about something, and he never feels guilty about women. Something's different."

Nina did not answer.

"You probably think I'm a worrywart." Kay stared out of the passenger window at the snow-covered fields.

"No, I think you're a paranoid old fool. A *private detective*? Kay, really. You've been reading too many mysteries."

"Nina, you don't know what it is to have a daughter like Charlotte. I'm only doing my duty as her mother."

"I told you what I think, and I'm not going to bang on about it. You seem to need to do this, so get your report and then let's drop all this arrant nonsense."

In January, Charlotte had time to write. *The Nutcracker* was over and rehearsals for *Firebird* didn't start until the end of the month. She bolstered herself up in bed with her laptop and wrote.

> "When I was sweet sixteen, I received an invitation from the Academie Princesse Grace in Monte Carlo to dance with their ballet students for a special event to be performed at the Palace in honor of Prince Rainier and Princess Grace's twenty-fifth wedding anniversary. The invitation came a year in advance, and as it turned out, the date coincided with spring break on the

next year's school calendar. Mother agreed that I could accept and planned for Lilly and Nina to accompany us on this hyper-luxurious, all-expenses-paid working vacation. The Hotel de Paris in Monte Carlo was to be our home away from home, and as you can imagine, all us girls were looking forward to this with great enthusiasm!

"Alas and alack, as it turned out Lilly would not be able to go. She'd been born with a twisted femur, and this had to be rectified. The surgeon was calling the shots, and he scheduled Lilly for surgery while I would be dancing in Monte Carlo. Nina stayed with Lilly, and Mother and I went alone to the heavenly principality.

"*Tender Is the Night* by F. Scott Fitzgerald was the assigned reading for spring break that year. The action takes place in the South of France, just over the border from Monaco, and I easily imagined myself to be Rosemary Holt, the teenage American movie star in the book. Dick and Nicole Diver are the main characters, and their daughter was called Topsy. I knew when I read that way back then that I would name my daughter Topsy, as well. I'm so thrilled to have my very own Topsy! I love her with all my heart and often think of that enchanted sojourn in Monaco. I tell her and tell her how lucky she is to have a name associated with such an outstanding book set in such a glamorous era.

"I own a first edition of the 1934 classic. I even had a leather box made for it to keep the original bright colors featured on the dust jacket in pristine condition. On the original dust jacket, the sky is a muted orange, so I asked the bookbinder to make the protective box that very color.

"Sitting here writing this book for you, Dear Reader, makes me long to reread *Tender Is the Night*. So I am going to take a break from writing and start reading it all over again tonight. The idea of taking up that book again has me tingling with anticipation. I can hardly wait to plunge into its pages and bathe in the magic of Fitzgerald's prose and my memories of the South of France!"

CHAPTER SEVEN

While Charlotte was re-reading Fitzgerald, Jack Harding was investigating Colin's activities. His job was easy as Colin never varied his routine, and Jasmine had never been discreet.

Several weeks later, back in Middleburg, Kay and Nina were having a cup of coffee in the wood paneled library after breakfast. Kay was sitting at a Sheraton desk reading the mail. Finally, she took her glasses off and turned to Nina.

"Did Charlotte ever tell you what Colin's bad investment was?"

"Security cameras, I think. Something about buying part of a company in Luxembourg or someplace." Nina was perusing the *Washington Post* on the faded chintz chaise longue.

"It's called Iris Security, and it's in Belgium. A retina scanning research company. Charlotte's fortune is in real jeopardy."

"You've heard from Jack Harding."

"Yes. He was very thorough. Colin's new girl, a Chinese woman, named Jasmine, works for an optometrist in the West Fifties from 8 to 3. And sees Colin after work."

"And?"

"Apparently her unusual services to one of this doctor's colleagues netted her over a million dollars in finder's fees. He was looking for investors in Iris Security, and she produced Colin with Charlotte's money. Jack says that Colin bought twenty percent of it in more or less good faith, knowing that Jasmine would get a fee, of course, but thinking it would be a good investment. Then there were huge sums required for development, and before Colin knew what hit him, most of Charlotte's money was required to fund additional development of a new technology."

"I'd never have believed he'd be so careless."

"It's not confirmed, but the pieces fit together very convincingly. And now, it seems even more money is needed if the company is going to stay afloat. Apparently, Colin is scrambling for other investors. Not looking good."

"What are you going to do with this information?"

"I don't know. I need your advice."

"Adam Holt is a brilliant businessman. His advice would be better than mine." Nina wondered if Kay noticed her blush when she said the name.

"Good idea. I feel up to a ride. Let's pay him a neighborly visit." Kay left her cup and saucer on the desk and went upstairs to change.

Kay and Nina saddled their horses and rode along the bridle path in the stinging cold ten miles to the beautiful white ante-bellum house, called Beech Hill, which had been in the Holt family for generations. Patches of snow littered a lawn stiff with frost, and tree skeletons sketched black graffiti on the white sky. They rode up the long, straight driveway flanked by live oaks, and by the time they'd dismounted, Adam Holt had opened the front door and was gesturing for them to come in. A groom materialized from nowhere and took the horses.

"Welcome to my two favorite neighbors! I'd have come on out and taken your horses myself, but as you can see, I'm only a little better than useless." Adam was on crutches and had a full leg cast. His thick white hair was tousled by the wind.

"What on earth happened to you?" Nina didn't sound worried, though her forehead was creased.

"Hunting accident. Don't ask. Surprised you haven't heard."

"We went to New York for Christmas, and then I had the damn flu. Been totally out of it for weeks," Nina said as they followed Adam into the formal living room. There was a fire blazing, books, newspapers and magazines scattered around. Adam sat down heavily in a wing chair with a kitchen stool in front of it for his leg. His wife of forty years had died three years previously, and the lack of a woman's touch was apparent.

Laying their hard hats on a side table, Nina and Kay made a beeline for the fire, taking off their gloves and holding their hands to the warmth.

"How about some coffee? Or would you like something stronger?"

"Coffee's fine." Nina tossed a newspaper on the floor and sat in an armchair near the widow, which looked out on the rose garden. The bushes were covered with tarpaulins, but the structure was defined. It had a harsh beauty.

"Nina, would you ring for Howard?"

Just at that moment, Howard appeared. "Miss Nina. Miss Kay. So glad to see you ladies. Mr. Holt, you'll be glad to know we have plenty of Brunswick stew, and I can set the table for three in a jiffy."

"Is it lunchtime all ready?" Adam looked up in surprise.

"No, sir. It's only 11:30, but you need some company around here."

"You bet I do. Hope you girls can stay."

"We'd be delighted," Kay said. "I need some advice."

Adam listened intently as Kay explained everything in Jack Harding's report, his bright blue eyes clouding over as the story got worse and worse.

"Kay, this is a very sticky wicket for you as a mother and mother-in-law, but legally, your son-in-law had every right to do what he did. It was dishonest and stupid, but legal. I'd advise you not to get involved. This sort of thing happens with tech companies. Research and development are expensive and many investors lose their shirts. Let your daughter and son-in-law work things out in their own way."

"And what about that Chinese woman? Was it legal for her to take Charlotte's money dressed up as a finder's fee?"

"It's legal, and I would leave it alone."

"You're probably right." Kay admitted.

"Colin's not worthy of Charlotte, but it's her call if she wants to stay with him after this or not." Adam was anxious to change the subject. "What did you girls do to amuse yourself in New York? I hope you went to see *Hamilton*."

"I'm sorry to say, we did not, but we did see Charlotte dance in *The Nutcracker*, which is always a special treat, and we hit most of the museums," Nina said.

"*Hamilton* is great. I want to see it again and would love to have you . . . and Kay join me."

On the ride back to Covert, Kay teased, "Oh, Nina, Nina, someone has a crush on you!"

Nina did not make one of her dry comebacks.

"Oh my God, you've got a crush on him, too. Let's invite him for supper tomorrow night, and I can stay in bed with a headache."

"We're in our seventies, for God's sweet sake."

"What? Do you think age is some kind of vaccine against love? It's not. You're never safe from it." Kay leaned down and patted the horse's neck.

"Oh, Kay. What do you know about love?"

"I know it when I see it. And it's beautiful at any age."

"I don't know where you get these ideas." Nina looked over at Kay.

"Just because you had a bad experience a lifetime ago, doesn't mean love is no good. It's so good it's sacred. And it's immortal. Often before I go to sleep, I think of Roy's love and sink in it while I drift off. It's seen me through some tough times. Dr. Karl Menninger said, 'Love cures. It cures those who give it, and it cures those who receive it.' I believe that. It's powerful stuff."

Nina was silent for the rest of the ride. As they were unsaddling the horses, she turned to Kay, "Okay. I'll call him. And you can have that headache."

"Make your meatloaf. And mashed potatoes."

"I was thinking of something less banal, like Beef Wellington."

"Meatloaf."

The sky was pregnant with waiting snow. Tiny flakes were just beginning to flutter down. As Kay and Nina made their way to the house, they could feel the icy kisses before they could see them. "Three inches expected tonight," Nina remarked.

The next night after dinner with Adam, Nina came to Kay's room, "You were right about the meatloaf."

"I'm right about a lot of things, and I think Adam's right for you."

"Right for me as a neighbor and friend."

"Don't completely shut down that narrow mind of yours, Nina."

"We'll see what happens. And thanks for having the headache."

Adam called the next morning to thank Nina for making his favorite meal and asked if she would join him at the Red Fox Tavern that night. He would pick her up at seven, if she were free. And of course Kay was welcome to come, if she were feeling up to it. Kay was not about to recover so soon, and Adam and Nina had a real date. Due to Adam's cast, however, Howard chauffeured them, and when Adam reached for her hand, Nina had a distinct feeling if they'd been alone, there would have been a kiss. Maybe two. She was surprised to admit to herself she would've liked that.

Kay was waiting up and would not let Nina pass her door without a full report.

"I feel kind of giddy, and I would've kissed that old geezer if Howard hadn't been holding the door for me." The bells were ringing in Nina's voice.

"This is so exciting! Now, you listen to me. Tomorrow you ride over to Beech Hill with some of that marmalade you made last month. You tell him what a good time you had and make sure you arrive around lunchtime. Or better yet, drive over there at teatime and stay for dinner. Stay till after Howard goes home."

"I can't do that."

"Of course you can. And will. It is a new world now, Nina. And it's your move. By the way, thanks for not saying, 'I told you so' about the detective."

CHAPTER EIGHT

Rehearsals for *The Firebird* were grueling, and Charlotte was showing signs of strain. She'd lost weight and was moodier than usual, complaining of headaches and constantly cold. Lilly and Priscilla began to worry. They couldn't help but notice she'd upped her consumption of Cheetos, M&Ms and Xanax. They wanted her to cut back on these things and start making an effort to get more protein.

"As soon as we go into stage rehearsals, I'll perk up. The studios are sort of dreary. And please stop with the nutritional advice. My body knows what it needs." Charlotte was stretching at the barre in her bedroom. Lilly and Priscilla were seated side by side on the small sofa near the fireplace. The fire was smoldering and needed stoking.

Lilly looked up over her glasses and lowered her embroidery hoop, "Charlotte, I'm going to insist on blood work. I want to see the numbers."

"I think what you want to see is Dr. Ellis. I know you've always had a crush on him. And I don't have time to go, you'll have to go for me."

"Oh, *please*. He hasn't the slightest interest in me, but he'll send a medical technician here to take the sample. I've already spoken to him. All you have to do is lie in bed and present your best vein."

Charlotte pulled her shawl tighter around herself and said, "I really appreciate your love and concern for me. I'll do it, but please don't expect me to change my eating habits or anything else while dancing *Firebird*. I couldn't take the stress."

Lilly and Priscilla caught each other's eye. What kind of response was this? Where was sarcastic and rebellious? They were worried now in earnest.

A few minutes later Lilly followed Priscilla to her office off the kitchen. "I'll call Dr. Ellis right now. This window of opportunity may never open again." Lilly already had her cell out and was searching for the number.

"She's too compliant. Something's wrong." Priscilla sat and shuffled through a stack of mail on her desk. "Have you noticed she's always cold now?"

"Overtired. I looked on the Internet and some of the side effects of Xanax include weight change, depression, and sexual problems, among other things. These also are symptoms of menopause. But at least, she doesn't seem to have trouble in the sex department."

Priscilla started to say something but changed her mind, and Lilly continued. "Charlotte was just saying the other day how attractive she still finds Colin even after all these years."

"Dr. Ellis would keep an eye on the amount of pills he prescribes. So she couldn't be abusing them, could she?" Priscilla turned and watched as Lilly paced the tiny room, finally sitting on the only other chair.

"She calls the hotel doctor every time we're on the road. She says she likes to meet them and find out whom they recommend for bones, just in case. She has done this for many years. I thought it was one of her quirks."

Lilly picked up a copy of *Harper's Bazaar*, started flipping through it as she spoke softly. "This spring when I was with her in Paris, she stopped in all the pharmacies. I thought nothing of it as she always came out with a barrette or a lipstick or a bag of marshmallows, but there might have been more to it than that. Benzos are less controlled there."

"How would you know something like that?"

"General knowledge." Priscilla shrugged.

"Now that you mention it, every time we've gone anywhere in Europe, she checks out every pharmacy. She makes jokes about it being her hobby to 'tour' as many as she can. I always thought she just liked looking around them, like I look around grocery stores." Lilly stood up still holding the magazine.

"You might say to Dr. Ellis there's a possibility she overdoes it, and maybe he can tell from the blood work if there is any reason for concern."

"There are so many laws now. It would be illegal for him." Lilly turned down a page of the magazine, closed it and placed it on Priscilla's desk.

"Think she'd sign a release?"

"Of course not. You know that." Lilly made an appointment for blood work on the following morning at 7:30. It had to be fasting blood. "Make a note for Gani not to send coffee up until the medical tech has left. I'll tell Charlotte, but she's apt to forget. In fact, that's another symptom. . . ."

"I'll come early and be here to open the door and show them up."

"Don't worry, Priscilla. I'm always up early. I'll come."

The next morning, Charlotte kicked up a big fuss. She hated needles, and her veins had always been hard to find. The poor tech was overwhelmed by the magnitude of the apartment and the eminence of the patient and somehow managed to stick her four times unsuccessfully before she told him in no uncertain terms to please leave.

It was up to Lilly to give him a cup of coffee and soothe him. "Mrs. Darling is not feeling well this morning. Normally, she's the sweetest of patients."

"I'm sorry I couldn't find a vein. I don't know what happened—I'm usually good at my job. Please tell her how sorry I am and how much I admire her."

Later that day, Lilly sent over two complimentary tickets for the dress rehearsal of *The Firebird* to the tech, with apologies from Charlotte and that was the end of blood samples.

A week later, Lilly made her own appointment with Dr. Ellis. "George, I'm so worried about Charlotte. She's showing signs of . . . I don't know what, but she's too thin and rather irritable." She felt self-conscious around him. If Charlotte had noticed she had feelings for him, perhaps he had, too.

“I can’t talk to you about her without her consent, Lilly. You’ve both been favorite patients for years, and I hope you know I care about both of you beyond the usual doctor/patient relationship. Get her to sign this, and we can talk.” He handed Lilly a single sheet of paper.

“I don’t want to involve Colin in this.”

“Right. And if she won’t sign, I might be able to make some other suggestions.”

Lilly folded the paper and slipped it into her bag. “I don’t have much hope that Charlotte will sign this. You know how she hates any disparaging comments about the nutritional values of Cheetos and chocolate. And she’d really hate you and me ganging up on her and advising different choices.”

“I talk to her about triglycerides, but she’s not interested.”

“I suspect there may be too many Xanax going down the gullet as well.”

“Try to get her to sign the release. I’d like to talk to you but can’t unless she signs.”

“You know, when she broke her shoulder, there were pain meds, too. She was very secretive about that, come to think of it.”

“How long ago was that? I’ve forgotten.” George shifted in his chair.

“Three years.”

“Dr. Klein, right?” George asked.

“Yes.”

“He’s a fine surgeon. Take that frown off your face, Lilly. Everything will be alright.”

The doctor walked Lilly to the door of his office and then to the door, which opened onto Park Avenue. He lingered there, watching her walk down the street, reluctant to let her out of his sight.

Lilly went straight to Charlotte's apartment and found her in the kitchen holding the Sub-Zero freezer door open, surveying the contents.

"Gani, what are these reduced fat Klondike bars doing in here?"

"They were out of the originals, Madame."

"Please give these away and get the originals. I only want the originals. The ratio of chocolate to vanilla is perfect. And full-fat ice cream is the only kind worth eating."

"I still have my coat on. I can go get them now, if you want." Lilly's cheeks were pink from the cold.

Charlotte turned from the freezer. "Oh, Lilly, I didn't know you were here."

"Now I'm on my way to get original Klondike bars. I could use one myself. Do they carry them at Madison Market?"

"They carry them especially for Madame, but they carry many varieties. Be careful," Gani warned.

"I'm a big fan of the originals, too. How many?"

"Two six-packs," said Charlotte.

"I can't believe we're thinking about ice cream on a day like this. I feel like a truant skipping school, and I have the distinct feeling that neither of us should be having them."

"Well, we'll eat them in the library with the door closed. No one can say anything because after all we *are* consenting adults." Charlotte closed the freezer door and blew a kiss to Lilly and headed for Priscilla's office.

"I'm back," she said to Priscilla. "Any calls?"

"Plenty. But the most important one is from your mother. She said to tell you Nina has a boyfriend."

"No way. Get her on the phone for me. Get either one of them on the phone." Charlotte noticed Priscilla had already made the call.

"Mrs. Pipes, Mrs. Darling for you." Priscilla handed the receiver to Charlotte.

"Nina! Tell me everything there is to know."

"Always remember this: your mother is never to be trusted with any information."

"I haven't even talked to her. So you have to tell me."

"I've had dinner a few times with Adam Holt. And now your mother has blown it up to be the romance of the century. It's nothing but two old farts banging back some calories together. Honestly, your mother should be a romance novelist."

"I remember Adam Holt. He's a handsome old dog."

"'Old' is the operative word. And you're as bad as your mother. I want to remind you, she and I are seventy-four, each, and Adam's seventy-seven. Just add that up, and you will know the number is too high for anything but friendship."

"Don't you believe it. Love doesn't give a damn about age. Remember what George Sand said? 'There is only one happiness in life, to love and be loved.' And Kahlil Gibran? 'When love beckons to you, follow him, though his ways are hard and steep.'"

"Stop! Your mother quoted all that to me this morning. Right after she read First Corinthians Chapter 13 and Shakespeare and Keats and countless others. What *is* it with you two?"

"We're just a couple of romantics, in love with love."

"God. Spare me."

"Are you happy, Nina?"

"Yes, I am. I really am."

CHAPTER NINE

On Valentine's Day, Charlotte had a two-pound heart-shaped box of Teuscher Champagne Truffles sent to every person involved with the ballet. Each box had a card signed, '*The Firebird*'. That came to three hundred pounds of Swiss chocolate delivered to the Lincoln Center rehearsal studios.

When the American Express bill came in, even Priscilla, who was accustomed to Charlotte's impulsive generosity and all sorts of extravagances, was amazed. "Mrs. Darling, I want to make sure this bill is correct. $37,950.49 for Teuscher?"

"What? Not possible. Get the calculator. I think they added a zero by mistake. I think they mean $3,790.49. Now, let's see there are one hundred and fifty people. Call Teuscher and find out how much per pound, and then tell them what's wrong with the charge. I sent the big hearts."

"Then I'm afraid that's right. Those chocolates are at least a hundred dollars a pound."

"Good grief. I had no idea."

"You need to check with me about prices." Priscilla was stern.

"I've been so busy and count on you for everything, Priscilla. Don't tell me I'm getting out of touch. I'm too young to be old."

"Well, it's too late to worry about it now."

"I sent mints at Christmas." Charlotte's voice was very small.

"But you had me do it, and I sent bouquets of candy canes. And if I'd been in charge this time, I would've sent Hershey's kisses. Everyone loves them."

"I don't know what got into me. I just thought of it, and the number is in my phone, so I called and didn't ask the price and just emailed the list. Don't tell anybody."

"Some people will have to know. Just leave the presents to me in future."

"I hate austerity. I would like to send chocolates to them every week. They're all so absolutely adorable."

"Most of them are dancers, Mrs. D. They watch their weight. You're the only one eating like you do. And if you weren't in constant motion, you'd be as big as a house."

"I know and the triglycerides. Good thing my metabolism is so high."

"That high metabolism isn't going to save you from diabetes. Please promise me you'll cut back."

Charlotte promised and halved her sugar consumption. She found it very stressful and compensated by supplementing her chemical intake with an additional half a Xanax in the afternoons accompanied by quite a few extra Cheetos and one extra Marlboro. That made eight cigarettes a day. Her goal was to cut back to three someday.

The success of *The Firebird* was unprecedented. Even the harshest critic admitted it was breathtaking in its beauty. Charlotte's face was all over New York. On busses, on subways. Clips of the ballet were on TV and in taxis. But she was working so hard, she was barely aware this was happening. It was the dancing itself that she loved. It was as if the fame meant nothing, and she carried on her highly disciplined routine, never missing a beat, and always striving for greater perfection.

A few days into sugar reduction, Charlotte dropped by Priscilla's office, and Priscilla said to her, "Your mother called to remind you that it's Nina's birthday tomorrow."

"Thanks, sweetie. Please send flowers and remind me to call her. I'm having trouble remembering anything outside the choreography."

"Will do," said Priscilla, and she did, but Charlotte forgot to make the call anyway. It was okay because of the flowers, but Priscilla noted this as being unusual even under the pressure of performance. It crossed her mind to mention this to Lilly, but she decided against it. A little slip-up like that was nothing compared to what else was going on. There were some other alarming numbers on the American Express bill, which had nothing to do with Teuscher.

Priscilla felt reasonably sure Charlotte didn't realize how obsessed Colin was with Jasmine. Priscilla was historically uninterested in Colin's affairs, but this one had taken on outlandish proportions. Starting with the December American Express statement, there were huge charges from luxury New York hotels.

The bill for February was on top of Priscilla's Lucite desk. She was now waiting for Colin to make his monthly visit to her office. She never sent bills to the bookkeeper for payment until he'd given the okay.

"Good morning, Priscilla. What have you got there?" Colin was wearing a gray cashmere overcoat and remained standing. He was frowning and seemed to be in a hurry.

"Mr. Stone, could you have a look at this?"

He gave the sheets of paper a cursory glance. "Yes, these charges are correct. They're steep, but since I don't have an office, I do my business in hotel suites. No reason to bother Mrs. Darling with any of this."

"Right," she said, looking down at the papers while Colin beat a fast retreat.

Charges from the Peninsula, the Four Seasons, the St. Regis and others made the chocolates look like nothing at all. Though usually the soul of discretion, Priscilla felt she had to broach the subject with Lilly.

She took a deep breath and phoned Lilly asking her to stop by the office. She found the December and January statements and placed them next to the February one in a neat row. Lilly arrived half an hour later with a cup of tea in her hand, steam curling up from the amber liquid.

“Mr. Stone said not to bother Mrs. Darling with this, but I thought you should know.”

Lilly gave a low whistle. “A few more months of this should just about wipe out the prudent reserve. I suppose there’s no mistake.” She settled into the chair to examine the bills.

“He approved the charges.”

“Can you copy these for me? And thanks for bringing it to my attention. When you called me, I thought it might be about the Teuscher bill. Charlotte told me about that one, but I see we have something much more serious here.”

Lilly’s phone rang as she was walking home. It was Kay. “Mom! I’m so glad to hear your voice. What news of the Middleburg love birds?”

“A lot of billing and cooing. I’d say it’s progressing nicely. What’s up with you?”

Lilly told her mother about Colin’s hotel expenses.

“I’m sure I know what that’s all about.” And Kay told Lilly what she had learned from Jack Harding, the detective. “I would’ve told you all this before, but Adam Holt said something that made me think twice. I don’t want to be a meddling mother, and Charlotte has known about the affairs for years. The money is gone. Adams says there’s no recourse.”

“But what do I do about this? Colin may have been naïve financially, but he’s stood by her side and played the part of adoring husband for thirty-two years. And he never drained the coffers like this before.” Lilly turned into her building, waving at the doorman on her way to the elevator.

“I’ll come and talk to him. We’ve always gotten along. I don’t want Charlotte to hear about this. She needs total concentration for Firebird.”

"Let me know your flight info, and I'll have a driver meet you. Will Nina come, too?"

"Certainly not. She's like a lovesick teenager. I'm expecting her to break out in zits any minute."

Lilly called Charlotte and told her their mother would be arriving the next afternoon. She sounded so pleased that Kay was coming and said the house seats for Firebird would be available. Charlotte was in a talkative mood and wanted to know all about Nina's romance. She ended by saying, "Let me go tell Priscilla that Mom's coming. I want everything to be just right."

Charlotte arrived at the apartment the following evening, and seeing the lights on in the library, she went in. Her mother and sister were sitting near the fire. "Mom! What a wonderful surprise! I didn't know you were coming."

Lilly was shocked. How could Charlotte have forgotten?

Later that evening, Lilly mentioned to Kay that Charlotte had been worrisomely forgetful recently. Kay gestured dismissively and said, "She's performing a very complicated and highly taxing dance in front of nearly three thousand people every night. It's only natural that she doesn't remember every conversation she has with you."

Lilly didn't agree and wondered if she should call Dr. Ellis, but she hadn't found the right moment to get Charlotte to sign the release. It was still in her bag getting more battered everyday.

Mother and son-in-law met at Le Vaucluse on East 63rd Street. Colin had no idea that a bomb was about to be dropped and came innocently, in a convivial mood.

The restaurant is the epitome of restrained elegance and is rightly known for its innovative French cuisine, the desserts especially exciting. Kay's personal favorite was the hot chocolate soufflé served with blackberry ice cream.

Their coats were whisked away, and they were ushered up the few steps, which divided the sleek dining rooms. The generous amount of space between tables ensured the luxury of relative quiet even in the midst of Manhattan.

Kay sat on a dark brown leather banquette facing Colin across the starched white linen cloth. They each ordered six of the oysters of the day with a glass of champagne and chatted about the romance budding between Nina and Adam.

Half an hour later, with their main courses in front of them and the waiter occupied elsewhere, Colin said, "Kay, it's a real treat to get you all to myself."

"You may not think so for long, as I want to discuss the American Express bill with you."

Colin leaned forward in his chair and put his forearms on the table. He raised his voice. "I may be wrong, but I don't think Charlotte and I need to have your approval for our credit card charges."

"Charlotte doesn't know, yet. But *you* know. You've seen the amounts and approved them."

"They come to very little more than the rent on my office which Charlotte shut down in a ridiculous overreaction to an adjustment to our investments. And in fact, hotels cost less, as I don't have any employees." Colin was pale with fury. "Not that this is any of your affair, and it's tax deductible since that is where I do business now."

"Are you delusional, Colin?"

"What do you mean? You know perfectly well what's deductible."

"Yes, I do and afternoons with Miss Jasmine Chong are not considered deductible by the IRS."

Colin managed to sputter, "Miss Chong is doing important research for me."

"Colin, this has gotten out of hand. You've put Charlotte's fortune in jeopardy, and now you're spending like a drunken sailor. All she has left is real estate."

"For your information Iris Security is working on some top secret technology that will be used by the military."

"I sincerely doubt it. I know the way things stand. What do you intend to do about it?"

"I'm not going to sit here and be insulted by you, for one thing. And for another, I'm going to move into the Carlyle and send the bill to Charlotte. I get half the proceeds for the sale of community property, don't forget." The decibel level of his voice was rising.

"Then half of the Carlyle bill will be coming out of your share. And half the mortgage payments. And half of the legal fees. It could take years to sell the properties. There could be nothing left. And let me remind you, Charlotte will still dance, and you have nothing at all to offer the world. And nothing at all to put on a CV." Kay's voice was low and controlled.

Colin pushed Kay's chair roughly on his way out, and shouted, "Meddling old bitch," into the hush of the stately restaurant.

He stalked out, oblivious of the stunned stares from staff and customers alike. He turned up his collar and hunched down against the March wind, striding back to 71st Street where he picked up his computer and told Priscilla to have all his clothes packed. He said he would let her know where to send them. He then marched across Central Park and let himself into Jasmine's apartment. It was small but neatly arranged with heavy 19th century Chinese furniture upholstered in blue satin, embroidered cushions everywhere. There was a trace of incense hanging in the air.

Colin poured himself a scotch and made himself comfortable on a low sofa near the window, which looked out onto Central Park, and by the time he heard her key in the door, he'd convinced himself that she would insist he move in with her. He would demure, and she would beg. He could see it all in his head.

Jasmine moved quickly towards the kitchen, her arms hugging two large grocery bags against her mink coat, which was the same color as her long straight hair. Her nose was running and her skin unusually pale. She didn't notice Colin right away, but when she did, her bland expression changed.

"What the hell are you doing here? I told you I'm having my Auntie for dinner tonight."

Colin told his tale. Jasmine listened in ominous silence.

He summed up, "And so here I am. All yours, my love."

She dropped the grocery bags on the floor and sprang on him with the fury of a hellcat, wrapping herself around him, her strong legs pinning him to the chair while she scratched at his face and bit him fiercely on the shoulder. Colin defended himself as best he could without harming her and was relieved to obey when he heard her shriek, "Get out! Get out, you repulsive snake." He felt the final kick as he slammed the door.

He narrowly missed a hospital stay and ended up at the Roosevelt Hotel on East 45th Street, negotiating a monthly rate with the manager. His scratched and bruised face did not present well, but the credit card was not denied, and Colin signed a six-month contract for a modest junior suite. Once settled, he texted Priscilla with the name of the hotel, adding that Charlotte could check in with her mother if she wanted details of his departure.

CHAPTER TEN

During this time of upheaval, Kay lived in the guest room at 740 Park, organizing everything from selecting the divorce lawyer to sewing buttons. She monitored what information got through to Charlotte. Kay had always known what to keep from Charlotte and what to discuss.

Charlotte was relieved to have her mother in charge. She had no stomach for conflict and wanted to remove herself from all decision making. In truth, she couldn't muster enough passion for Colin to care what happened one way or another.

The tabloids spilled a lot of ink on this divorce. They provided the drama, and pictures of Colin and Jasmine appeared everywhere. Colin was interviewed on talk shows, and to his credit, he didn't belittle Charlotte. He talked on and on about the happiness he'd found with Jasmine and their plans for a future together. Charlotte tuned in only once. Seeing Colin acting like a teenager in love was more than she was willing to take. She picked up the remote, aimed it at him and emphatically pressed 'Power Off,' screwing up her mouth to show her disapproval. Not nearly as satisfying as throwing something heavy, but she restrained herself.

For her part, Jasmine was delighted with the notoriety and asked Colin to live with her. She fanned interest with incendiary comments about *The Firebird* on Facebook with a Charlotte-can-please-an-audience-but-not-a-man theme, claiming she didn't have to steal Colin since Charlotte had driven him into her arms, where he was now ecstatically happy and sexually satisfied with many more than fifty shades of gray.

She had another theme as well. She branded Charlotte a hypochondriac so obsessed with her health that it verged on insanity, adding that she saw masses of doctors on a monthly basis and was fueled by numerous prescription drugs.

What Jasmine didn't know was that none of this caused Charlotte the faintest irritation as she never even peeked at social media. Priscilla handled it all. After a few months of not getting a rise out of Charlotte, Jasmine gave up these themes. Charlotte was spared from whatever hurt she might have felt or whatever insights she might have drawn from these strangely close to home comments. Fortunately, none of Charlotte's friends or family or fans took anything Jasmine posted seriously.

Photographers loved Jasmine and couldn't get enough of her in provocative postures. She didn't interview well on film, though. On her first interview, she was anxious to steal the show and continually interrupted Geraldo, laughing too often and too loudly, making large gestures, which blocked him from the camera. As hard as Colin tried to promote her, she was never invited back by any of the networks.

Charlotte, on the other hand, was carefully managed by Kay, Lilly and her PR team. She never put a foot wrong. Her behavior was always gracious and dignified. Topsy was the wild card. Hating Jasmine was a given. She'd never sided with her mother on anything, but this time, she vacillated between Colin and Charlotte. Topsy never thought it through or accepted that it was her father's decision to put all the capital into Iris Security, which had put her mother in such difficulties in the first place. Kay wasted her breath in explaining this over and over to the PhD candidate, who had no intention of understanding or forgiving her mother for being famous.

In the middle of all this publicity and personal distress, the General Director of the Bolshoi Ballet came to New York, where he naturally attended several performances of *The Firebird.* The real purpose of his visit was to invite Charlotte to Moscow to dance *Giselle* with his company. Giselle isn't in City Ballet's repertoire, and Charlotte had never danced it.

She was pleased with the honor and grateful that her mother and Lilly would make it all happen without her involvement. She never avoided rigorous work and looked forward to throwing herself into the project. She loved a new role, and this was a great opportunity to bury herself in training. A wonderful excuse not to notice what was happening around her.

Lilly negotiated the terms, and the Bolshoi agreed to pay for a private coach. Charlotte would rehearse in New York, then arrive in Moscow, with her coach plus three others, ten days in advance to rehearse with the Bolshoi. All that was left for Charlotte was to sign the contract. The signing was to take place in the Director's suite at the St. Regis Hotel. Kay would meet Charlotte there.

Charlotte didn't show up. She'd completely forgotten.

It wasn't an international incident only because Kay handled it with the greatest of care. The Director was red with anger, when after waiting for a half an hour, Charlotte still hadn't appeared. Kay picked up the phone for room service and ordered Champagne, then looked down at her phone and pretended to answer it.

"Yes, Charlotte. . . . Oh, my dear, how dreadful. I'll come to the hospital right away. . . . Don't worry. He's right here beside me. Of course he'll understand."

She turned to the bewildered Russian and said, "There has been a taxi accident. Please forgive me, but I have to go to the hospital. Give the papers to me and I will have them signed and delivered back to you this evening. Thank you for your kindness and understanding."

She left the suite just as the Champagne was arriving. The Director seemed pleased to be called kind and understanding and to have the whole bottle to himself.

Later that afternoon, back at Charlotte's apartment, Lilly told her mother, "She's losing it. She's taking too many pills."

"Don't be silly. Not many people could stand up under this extreme pressure. She's doing a great job. She's in constant pain and all this stress around the divorce takes its toll, you know."

"There have been a lot of things she forgets lately, Mom. And she's always cold and tired. I think we have to do something."

"Your sister is highly strung. Don't interfere. I'd know if something were wrong."

"She didn't even remember you were coming to New York. She practically went to sleep during lunch, and if there weren't so many of us hounding her all the time, I think she would forget to shower. Hygiene seems to be getting lower in her list of priorities."

"Don't be ridiculous. I think she's totally amazing considering all the factors, including divorcing her husband of thirty-two years, dealing with financial chaos, dancing *The Firebird*, coping with Topsy, smiling for photographers. Not to mention, talking to journalists and ignoring what they write while planning on dancing with the Bolshoi. Each of these things is major. Leave her alone."

"I can't leave her alone. Yesterday she almost left the apartment with a filthy blouse on."

"A one time oversight."

"Okay, if you say so, but I'm keeping score now," Lilly said emphatically.

"Forget about keeping score and start thinking about who's going to train her for *Giselle*," Kay said.

"It has to be someone adept with pantomime. It's a very particular ballet. Alexandra Danilova used to be the one to go to," Lilly replied, her mind now focused on the task at hand.

"Find out who took her place. Opening night in Moscow is a year from today. She'll have to study for six or seven months at least. Maybe Gail Kirk would coach her."

"I bet she will. Being invited by the Bolshoi is a high honor indeed."

"The highest. Charlotte has to be perfect. And find someone for Russian lessons, too. She needs to master the basics. We should do that with her." Kay thought of everything.

"Are you back for good now, Mom? Shall I retire?"

"Of course not, Lilly, but this is a life crisis, and I need to be with her until she settles down after the divorce. I'm here as her mother, not her manager."

"Could've fooled me."

"You weren't with us when she danced Petrouchka at the Mariinsky in St. Petersburg. Prima ballerinas are like rock stars in Russia. She must be prepared to say charming things in Russian on TV. With a credible accent. Let's get the language lessons going right away."

"The Bolshoi contract doesn't include Russian language lessons."

"I'll pay."

Even if Lilly was annoyed, she acknowledged her mother was impressive. And right. She called around and found Dmitri Shumakov, who, for the next year, would be having breakfast with them five days a week.

Pitchers of fresh orange juice and pots of hot coffee would be available every morning as well as yogurt and granola. Some people would probably have bacon and eggs, and others would insist upon eating Cocoa Puffs or Captain Crunch.

When Dmitri walked in, Charlotte recognized him right away as one of Balanchine's friends. He was unforgettable at six-foot-four with a beautifully shaped shaved head. He was handsome, although a bit over-fed. She'd seen him on a trip she'd made to New York with some others in the Washington Corps de Ballet in 1982. Balanchine was dying in Roosevelt Hospital then, and a City dancer told her that Dmitri went with Mikhail Baryshnikov to a restaurant in Brighton Beach every day to get sustenance for him. Balanchine couldn't take the hospital food. All he wanted was stuffed mushrooms from Skovorodka.

She didn't mention this to Dmitri. He would never have remembered a young ballerina from Washington visiting the big city. She guessed he was about ten years older that she was and decided not to put him through the indignities of having to act out the charade of remembering her.

She let his booming voice spill over her. She would have recognized that voice anywhere and was inspired to be his pupil.

* * *

Adam Holt was out of his cast in time for the last hunt of the season, and since he was Master of Foxhounds, the members of the hunt met at Beech Hill that day at nine, followed by a gala hunt breakfast at Covert. Although Kay was still in New York, Nina had everything in hand and was ready to ride, but there was a small fire in her kitchen caused by frying chicken. Nina had to assess the damage and was unable to join the hunt.

Lola O'Sullivan had not been in Middleburg for at least a decade, but she showed up booted and spurred and superbly mounted. On top of that, she was using her grandmother's sidesaddle and wearing her habit with the robin's egg blue collar. She was Charlotte's age, and they had known, and not liked, each other as girls. During the course of the hunt, it became apparent to the whole field that it was Adam, not the fox, she was after. At seventy-seven, he was flattered that an able-bodied blond of fifty-three would find him a suitable quarry, but he appeared uninterested, at first.

Relentlessly, Lola pushed hunt etiquette to the limit and was practically riding abreast of Adam. She knew she should be behind the Master, but she also knew her place was secure. Her father and grandfather had been Masters of the Middleburg Hunt, and no one would dare reprimand her. Especially, considering how proficient and resplendent she was riding sidesaddle, a dangerous and practically lost art. Nina was probably the only other woman in the Commonwealth of Virginia who could compare equestrian skills with Lola.

The members of the hunt arrived at Covert at noon. No trace of the fire was evident and Nina was at the door with a platter of miniature quiches, and beside her stood two of her former pupils holding trays of mint juleps. The dining room table was laden with two Smithfield hams, baskets of piping hot biscuits, tureens of cheese grits as well as crispy bacon, broiled tomatoes, and fried chicken. No kale or quinoa anywhere to be seen.

Lola made a grand entrance, hugging Nina to her and saying in a loud voice, "I should have been right here helping you, Miss Nina, instead of riding hell bent for leather. You should've seen Adam. He's a genius at leading the Field. Oh my, you look so frail, let me take that platter for you."

"Why, Lola, dear, how lovely to see you."

"I've been living in Ireland, as you've probably heard, and I got to know that Kevin McGettigan of yours. Old Green Eyes, they call him. Still chasing skirts at eighty or whatever he is. A total alcoholic wreck, though, so he doesn't have much success." Lola did not make a move to take the hors d'oeuvres from Nina, who was flushed with anger.

Lola continued, "On the other hand, a good specimen, like Adam here, will always have great success with the ladies, won't you, Adam honey?"

"Now, Lola, why would you say a thing like that?" Adam was all smiles.

"Just watching you take control today made me proud to be a Virginian. Irishmen think they know all about horse flesh, but nobody knows more about a fox than you."

"Well, I've been hunting the fox a long time, and I know this country inside out. Plus, our hounds are the best in the state."

Lola poked Nina in the ribs. "Listen to Adam. Isn't he perfection?"

Nina was blindsided. She took the platter of hors d'oeuvres upstairs to her bedroom. No one seemed to notice she'd disappeared, and muffled laughter filtered through to her as she lay on top of her bed stiff and still. Finally, she reached for the phone and dialed Kay's cell.

"Kay, listen. I'm coming to New York on the next plane. I don't want to explain until I see you. Do you think it would be all right with Charlotte if I stay there? If not, I can stay with Lilly."

Kay didn't quiz her. "Of course, stay here. We just started Russian lessons the other day. Our teacher descends from a cavalry officer in the Czar's Imperial Guard and looks like he came straight from central casting."

"Just hearing your voice cheers me up, my friend. I'll be there in time for dinner."

Nina hung up and explained to one of the helpers that she was needed in New York. Someone would clean up and lock up after the guests left, and one of the grooms drove her to Dulles airport.

Safe in the green and white guest room, Nina let herself go. Kay held her hand as the story, what there was of it, poured out with her tears. She ended by saying, "I slipped out the back door and peeked through the screened porch, and there stood Adam and Lola, laughing their fool heads off. He hasn't even phoned me to ask what happened."

Before Kay had a chance to say anything, Nina's phone rang. They both looked at the screen, then at each other. "Let it go to voicemail," Kay said.

"Don't tell the girls about my little old heartache. I'm embarrassed at my age to not be above, beyond and over such silliness, and I hate that I left myself open for this. I should have learned my lesson all those years ago and not go playing with fire again."

"Stop this, Nina. It's only five-thirty. And Adam has tried to call you already. He would have stayed at the breakfast until the bitter end and then would've had to see to the hounds and his horse. So he couldn't have gotten home much before five. He's had a shower and is now calling you to see what took you to New York in such a hurry. Go ahead and listen to the message."

Nina put the phone on speaker and Adam's voice filled the room, "Hey, Nina. Sorry you had to leave your own party. I hope everything's okay. You really missed a good time. Lola spins a great tale and entertained us all with stories of Ireland. You'll be happy to know she'll be hunting with us next season. She missed Middleburg and is coming back to us.

"Give me a call and let me know how long you'll be in New York. I'm going out for dinner but should be home by ten or so."

"Ouch," Nina said.

"Call him in the morning and say there was a false alarm about my health. We'll have to strategize and decide whether it's better for you to go home right away and defend your territory or better to stay here and have him wonder."

"I can't defend my seventy-four year old self from Lola. You should see her."

Kay put her arm around Nina's shoulders. "Come on. We're going for a walk. Very cheering for girls of any age to window shop in New York." They sailed down Madison Avenue with the wind at their backs.

CHAPTER ELEVEN

Charlotte, Kay, Lilly and Nina were seated in Charlotte's breakfast room the following morning. The yellow curtains were glowing in the spring sunshine, and the canaries were singing. Everything was bright and shiny, except Nina's sad face. Charlotte had gotten home too late to see her the previous evening and had only had a text from Kay saying that she was coming.

"I'm delighted you're here, Nina. I hope you'll stay for a while and learn Russian with the rest of us. We have such a handsome teacher."

"*Privet, deti*!" Dmitri stormed in with his big arms open wide.

"*Privet*, Dmitri," Charlotte answered.

"Oh, my! Another beautiful pupil for me."

"This is our dear friend, Nina Pipes," Charlotte said.

"Welcome to our Russian breakfast club." Dmitri brought her hand to his lips. "And now to work." He passed out sheets of paper. The page was titled, "Interesting Adjectives".

An hour later Nina had some color back in her cheeks and was ready to go with Kay for a walk around the reservoir in Central Park. As they were passing behind the Metropolitan Museum, they came face to face with Colin, his tall, slim torso slumped over.

"Kay. Nina. Good morning."

"I certainly hope you're happy." Kay's voice was severe.

"I'm not, if it makes you feel any better. I'm miserable." The wind tossed his brown curls. He looked young and vulnerable, not at all like the angry man who'd shouted at her in the restaurant.

"A natural consequence of your actions, Colin," Kay said as she turned to continue her walk. Nina raised her hand in parting but said nothing.

Once on the track, Nina said, "Colin looks as gloomy as I feel. Isn't it funny how love can bring such happiness and such pain? Both leave me breathless."

"Call Adam back when you're sure he won't answer."

"Why? What's the message going to be?"

"You'll know what to say when you hear the beep."

They took two laps around the reservoir and arrived on 71st Street in time to run into Charlotte in the lobby. "Nina, Adam Holt called my landline looking for you. He wanted to know what was wrong. I didn't know what to say. I said everything had resolved itself. I hope that was the right answer."

Nina's brow relaxed in relief. "You go to the head of the class. That was the perfect answer. I'll give him a call later."

In the elevator, Kay said, "You see? He's worried about you."

A few minutes later in her room, Nina answered her cell. Adam said, "Hey, just checking to see if everything's okay and when you're coming back."

"Everything's fine. There was a false alarm about Kay. I might stay here a bit longer, though."

"How long, do you think?"

"I'm not sure. Why?"

"Well, Lola invited me to Hobe Sound for Easter, so if you're not coming back, I'll go with her."

Nina blanched and raised her voice, "Can't hear you, Adam. Lots of static on the line. Will have to call you back."

Nina cut the connection, repeated the conversation to Kay, then said, "This is not what I'd hoped for, in case you're wondering."

"Look. Charlotte can call him and invite him to go with us to Palm Beach. She doesn't know about any of this, and the invitation will sound perfectly natural."

Charlotte made the call saying that her mother and Nina always had Easter with her in Palm Beach and asking him to join them this year. His reply was evasive, and Charlotte had to say, "Adam, is that a 'Yes' or a 'No'?"

He cleared his throat and said, "It's a 'Yes'. I accept your invitation with great pleasure." He didn't sound pleased at all, and that evening Charlotte said to Kay, "Adam's a strange bird, isn't he?"

"What do you mean?"

"When I invited him, you would've thought I was inviting him to Gitmo, not Palm Beach. He sounded like there were a hundred better invitations he was giving up to please me."

"He's just old and losing his charm. Nina's going to stay in New York until we go to Florida."

Kay reported to Nina. "Adam's coming. He's delighted to be invited, but he should suffer a little, so don't return his calls. Text him that you're busy. You'll see him soon enough."

Charlotte's house on Middle Road in Palm Beach was designed by Maurice Fatio, a famed Swiss architect who created many of the most beautiful houses built in Palm Beach during the 1930s. Charlotte had the stucco painted a pale blue with the shutters and trim gleaming white. A bay window jutted out on the south side of the façade and a fragrant pink climbing rose framed the wide front door, which was topped by a narrow balcony. On the east side was a coral rock terrace, which overlooked a deep blue pool. Beyond the pool, four grapefruit trees displayed their yellow orbs in front of a charming gazebo, the back wall of which was incrusted with shells in a geometric design.

It was a lovely house and Charlotte hated losing it, but this feeling of loss and her anger at Colin were mitigated by various chemicals. She'd never liked feeling sentimental or angry or resentful or anything at all, actually. She preferred the serenity of numbness.

Now that her divorce was under way, the house was on the market, and this might be their last Easter on Middle Road. Topsy was so mad when she heard the house was for sale, she refused to come. "You're cutting off your nose to spite your face, dear," her grandmother told her.

The ballet season was over until fall, and Charlotte had decided not to go with the Company to Saratoga this summer. Months of relative rest stretched before her. She was delighted to be in Palm Beach, lazing in the sun, swimming laps in her pool and having Peggy Elliot's special pedicures. Kay was happy in the garden, and Gani loved shopping with Lilly at the green market. It was Nina who was off kilter. Adam was arriving the next day around noon.

"Kay, come with me to Worth Avenue. I want to go to Neiman's or Saks and have a makeover." Nina's voice was strained.

"I want to come, too," Lilly said.

Charlotte waved good-bye to the three of them saying, "Thank God I can have a few weeks without makeup." She picked up *Essentially Lilly,* a book by Lilly Pulitzer on entertaining in Palm Beach, and sank into a plush sofa on the loggia to peruse the photographs. She heard the gravel crunching and then the doorbell rang.

Moments later Gani came in. "Madame, Dr. Ellis is here."

"Oh my goodness, George. How nice to see you. Did I know you were coming? Did Lilly send you to take my blood?"

"No. I'm here for a week and was out walking and saw all the cars so I thought you wouldn't mind if I stopped by."

"Of course not. The rest of the family is out stirring up the economy on Worth Avenue, but please come in and have some iced tea or sugar-free lemonade."

"I won't stay, but if I can have your number, I'll call and invite you all out to lunch or dinner."

Charlotte wrote down the number and saw him to the door. That's weird, she thought, and then forgot.

Nina, Kay and Lilly came back with bags and bags from Saks and Neiman's but too tired to go out and show off their beautifully made up faces. They had an early supper on the terrace and were just saying goodnight when the phone rang.

It was Adam saying that he was not feeling well and would not be joining them. He told this to Charlotte, adding at the last minute, "Please tell Nina how sorry I am, and how much I was looking forward to seeing her."

Even before Charlotte had taken her hand off the receiver, it rang again. This time it was George Ellis wanting Charlotte to pick a day and time. "How about lunch tomorrow? But let's make it here. One o'clock."

Everyone was waiting to hear who'd called. Charlotte thought Nina was not as disappointed as expected and noted that the news had a positive effect on Lilly.

The following morning they were having breakfast on the terrace. Charlotte said, "You know who I miss? Dmitri. Why don't we invite him down for a Russian language bender? It would be great, *Russie-sur-mer*."

This idea was greeted with enthusiastic approval. A call was made, an invitation accepted.

Nina said to Kay, "I'm glad we're going to immerse ourselves in Russian. I need to stop nursing my dashed hopes and dreams and let them go forever. I should've known better than to believe in love at seventy-four. You know, I disapprove of self-pity, and here I am the worst culprit."

"He's the loser."

"Everyone says that to the ditched. But thanks."

"You know, Nina. Why don't you give Adam the benefit of the doubt? He may be in Middleburg and not feeling well. You don't know for sure he went to Hobe Sound with Lola."

"I'm alright, Kay. Disappointed, that's all."

George Ellis arrived spot on time. He was tan, which made his blue eyes look almost turquoise. Luncheon was served by the pool, but before dessert, Gani came to Nina and said, "Mr. Holt's butler is on the phone for you."

Nina raced for the phone. The nearest one was in the pantry. "Howard?"

"Miss Nina, I got some bad news. Mr. Holt's in the hospital. He was all set to go see you in Florida yesterday but didn't feel up to it. Then this morning he had a little heart attack. The ambulance took him to Stone Springs. He doesn't know I'm calling, but I thought you should know."

"I'm coming right away."

"Let me know what time, and I'll be waiting at baggage claim."

"Okay, Howard, and thanks for calling me. Warn Mr. Holt that I'm coming."

Kay was standing beside Nina when she got off the phone, and when she heard what happened, she said, "I'm going with you."

"You don't have to. Howard will meet me and take me to the hospital."

"Go pack, Nina. And put in a few things for me. I'll ask Lilly to make the reservations."

George wanted to know the details, but there weren't any, so he called the hospital and was able to get the name of Adam's doctor. It was Ben Toler whom Nina and Kay both knew, but the hospital could give no other information. He was not able to reach Ben, but the office assured him Adam was in good hands and in stable condition.

"Thank you, George, for calling. Nina was in shock and didn't ask a single question," Kay said. She kissed Lilly and Charlotte, and took Nina by the arm and hurried her to the waiting taxi.

Nina was silent in the taxi and on the plane. Her heart went from fear to hope and back again. Kay patted her hand and left her to her thoughts. One minute Nina's mind was building a life with Adam and the next she was mourning him at the grave. By the time the plane touched down at Dulles, Nina was an exhausted wreck.

She came right back to life when she saw Howard waiting for them. He greeted them warmly and carried their bags to Adam's Jeep Cherokee. On the way to the hospital Nina said, "Howard, I hope Miss O'Sullivan won't be there."

"Oh, no, Ma'am. She's gone back to Ireland. A man they called McGettigan Junior came and got her a few days back. Mr. Holt and me, we were mighty glad to see her go."

"You were?"

"Yes, Ma'am. She was getting on our nerves."

CHAPTER TWELVE

The next morning, Charlotte was in the kitchen munching a handful of Cheetos. "Gani, on your way home from Publix, please stop by Green's and get some Clark bars and half a dozen Reese's Peanut Butter Cups, but only get the Easter ones. They're egg-shaped. They have a much better proportion of peanut butter to chocolate than the regular ones. Please be careful to get only those. I hate to waste the calories on the round ones."

"Yes, Mrs. Darling, I remember from previous years. Those eggs are in season now."

"After that, go to Lewis's and get two bags of Haribo gummy dinosaurs. Don't get the frogs by mistake. They're too sweet. And charge my account. Be careful coming home. Lilly can't see you with them. And whatever you do, if you talk to Priscilla, don't mention it. Bring everything to my room and put it under the bathroom sink."

"But, Madame, Dr. Ellis is in town."

"Well, don't mention it to him, either. It's Easter weekend, and I've been so good."

"How many for dinner tonight?"

"Only Lilly and me, I think. But just in case, you'd better go to Mildred Hoit and pick up a tin of Betsy's Cheese Straws. You never know, someone might drop in. Lilly says no one eats Cheetos, except me."

Lilly came in the kitchen at that moment and said, "That's not right. I said no *adults* eat Cheetos except you, and no one wears sweaters in south

Florida in springtime except you, either. It's 80 degrees. What are you doing with that sweater on?"

"I just got out of the pool. I'm cold."

As it turned out, Charlotte was alone for dinner as George had asked Lilly out. He took her to Café l'Europe and after dinner they walked on the beach back to Middle Road. Silhouetted against the evening sky, the palm fronds did a slow dance in the soft breeze, and the two New Yorkers reveled in the tropical night air.

Once they arrived at Charlotte's house, Lilly drove George back to his car on South County Road. Then George followed Lilly home to make sure she got there safely but was too shy to kiss her.

Late the next afternoon, Charlotte was asleep in the sun when suddenly the large shadow of Dmitri loomed over her. For a moment she didn't know who he was or why he was there. She recovered quickly and managed, "*Privet*, Dmitri! And welcome."

"Ah, my *myshka*, alone at last!"

The tenderness in his voice triggered her fear of intimacy like an electric shock.

Too loudly, she said, "Mom and Nina have gone to Virginia, so it's just Lilly and me."

For the rest of the stay in Palm Beach, Lilly watched Charlotte avoid Dmitri. She did her best hide this from Dmitri, but he knew. Of course he knew.

A week later in the country hospital in Virginia, Adam Holt admitted to himself how content he was that Nina was a constant visitor. His experience with Lola made the thought of a younger woman unappealing to him. Lola had irritated him with her restlessness and her constant need for attention. And she got a little nasty after a few gin martinis. Nina was just the tonic he needed, and he wondered if he needed to apologize about Lola or not. It was too difficult a decision, so he let it ride.

Nina had been stunned to see Adam so weak and pale. His powerful body appeared to have shrunk since she'd last seen him, but she never let her concern show. And she, like Adam, never could bring herself to discuss Lola.

Nina and Kay were in Adam's hospital room, and Nina asked, "When are you going to get your lazy self out of this place? I'm sick of the view."

"I've been telling Ben that I would recover much quicker at home."

Ben Toler entered the room in time to hear this. "If you weren't such an ornery old fool, I'd release you with the proviso that someone spend the night with you in that big old house of yours. But we've had this conversation about your independence before, so I'm keeping you here a while longer."

"Nina and I can take turns with him, Ben," said Kay.

"In that case, I'll reconsider, but one of you has to be there when Howard goes home at night, every night. I don't want this buzzard left on his own for a while yet. He needs to take it easy."

It was settled, and both Nina and Kay had dinner on trays with Adam in his bedroom at Beech Hill that night. The room was incongruously feminine with a frilly dressing table and flowered silk curtains. Evidently there'd been no redecorating in quite some time.

Since it was Adam's first night out of the hospital, both women decided to stay to get used to the house. Howard had had all the rooms aired and made up so they had a choice. Eventually, they decided on the two nearest Adam and installed a baby monitor in his room despite his loud objections.

The next morning, Adam insisted on getting dressed and coming downstairs for breakfast. Before long he was the color of the napkins, and Howard had to settle him in bed without finishing the omelet.

Nina said she had some errands to run but would return on horseback in time for dinner, and at 4:30 she mounted Prancer, her favorite mare, and rode to Beech Hill in the fading light. The protean sky was swirling with pink, purple and scarlet. She could feel the pulse of spring in the air and a nascent joy in her heart.

For the first week Nina and Kay both had dinner with Adam and alternated spending the nights at Beech Hill. Then Kay said, "Charlotte and Lilly are back in New York, and I need to get there to keep everything on track. You're in charge of Adam now."

Nina and Adam didn't resume the same closeness that they'd had earlier in the year. Whether that was due to the Lola episode or to Adam's health, Nina wasn't sure, but one morning Nina was early for breakfast and couldn't help but notice a letter postmarked Dublin on top of Adam's mail. This letter from Lola was not mentioned by either of them.

Three weeks later, just as they were beginning to unwind and relax around each other, Ben Toler came for dinner in the capacity of friend, not doctor.

"Nina, you and Kay have done such a good job with our patient that he's as strong as an ox. You'll be relieved to know, he can stay alone now."

Nina and Adam avoided glancing at each other. Both thought the other would be delighted with this news. Covering up his disappointment, Adam said, "I'm sure Nina would like you to give her a ride home, Ben. She's my favorite nurse, but she's been on duty a long time."

"Wait a moment, Ben. I'll pack my things and be right down." Nina forced her voice to sound cheery.

Adam was matter-of-fact as he said good-bye, giving her a dry peck on the cheek. Adam said, "I'll ride Prancer over to Covert around noon tomorrow, if you'll give me lunch and drive me home."

It was a little after ten that night when Nina opened the front door of Covert and waved good-bye to Ben Toler. She switched on the lamps, but they failed to dispel the gloom. Leaving them all on, she made her way up to her bedroom.

Kay called the next morning. "I hope you'll be bringing our patient to Newport for the sea air."

"I don't think he gives a damn about the sea air or me, Kay." There was a catch in her voice, and Kay's heart lurched with compassion. "Last night Ben said he could stay alone now, and Adam couldn't wait to get rid of me. Even suggested Ben take me home right away."

"I see the way that man looks at you. He just doesn't know how to express himself. Keep an open mind, Nina."

"I'd like to get out of town. Are you still in New York?"

"Yes, we're not leaving for Newport until Friday."

"I'm going to come this afternoon. Adam's riding Prancer over this morning and is expecting lunch, but I'd like to leave as soon as possible. I don't want to spend another night here alone."

Adam was all set. He put the ring in a green leather pouch. It had been his mother's, and he had given it to Annie, his wife, when his mother died, he had never seen her wear it. It was an oval ruby surrounded by old mine cut diamonds. Old fashioned, even for a woman of Nina's age, but he thought she would like it.

He rode on the bridal path in the May splendor, thinking what a lucky man he was. After putting Prancer in the capable hands of the women running Nina's stable, he made his way through the apple orchard to the house.

Nina opened the door. "Adam, I hope you don't mind a sandwich. I'm headed to New York this afternoon. I don't expect to be back much before mid-September."

Adam managed to keep his face neutral. "A sandwich is fine, Nina. I appreciate all the time you and Kay spent with me. I realize I've kept you from a lot of exciting things."

"Not really, but it's going to be too hot here any day now."

After an awkward lunch, Nina said, "One of the girls will drive you home. I'm going in the other direction. Glad you're feeling so well. Let us know if you are coming to New England. I'm sure Charlotte would love to have you stay."

"Newport's not my thing. Have a good summer, and I'll be here when you get back in the fall." Adam turned away sadly.

Nina arrived on 71st Street in the lavender twilight with heavy suitcases. She had no intention of going back and forth to Middleburg. Charlotte's Newport place had a pool house with two guest rooms, which she had given over to Nina and Kay years ago. Of course the house was on the market, and who knew what would happen, but it didn't seem like an active real estate market this year if you could judge by Palm Beach. No one had come to see the house on Middle Road for months.

Lilly had been busy negotiating a new contract for Charlotte and had not been free the one and only night George Ellis invited her for dinner since they'd returned to New York. She asked him to escort her to a party at the Consulate General of Italy. They were having a dinner dance in honor of a fashion designer who was enamored with Charlotte. George had said 'yes' but then had an emergency at the last minute. He told Lilly to have a nice summer and that he would look forward to seeing her when she returned.

Mario Buatta escorted Kay and Charlotte, but in the end, neither Nina nor Lilly could be persuaded to go with them.

The air was nippy when they arrived in Newport, but the smell of the salt air and the cry of the gulls were a balm to the four women when they arrived at Charlotte's. It was a rambling early 20th century weathered shingle cottage with crisp white trim, named Seventh Heaven. The garden was missing the annuals, but other than that, everything was ship-shape.

"Charlotte, Nina and I will stay in the house with you and give the pool house to Dmitri. We don't want to fuel the tabloids," Kay said as they were getting out of the van which had met them at the airport.

"Better, yet, let's get him a room at Hotel Holly. I think it's better that he isn't staying at Seventh Heaven," Lilly commented.

"He has lots of friends here. I'm sure he would prefer staying at Holly's. I should've thought of that in the first place," Charlotte said. "But Holly is so fussy about who she lets her rooms to. Is he socially registered enough for her?"

"Dmitri has plenty of charm. Holly will love him, but if he's not staying here, I think the lessons should start promptly at nine and go through lunch. Charlotte, you need to knock their socks off in Moscow." Kay would make sure of that.

Lilly said, "Well, I don't have to impress anyone with my command of Russian, and I hate to break it to you beauties, but I'm going to spend two months on Long Island. I heard this morning that a little salt box in Sag Harbor has lost its renter, and I'm moving in."

"Lilly, what fun! I'm coming to visit. I've never been to that part of Long Island, and I'm dying to go." Nina liked Newport, but not as much as the others did.

It was decided that Nina and Kay would have the pool house, as usual. Dmitri would stay at the very posh bed and breakfast, Holly Court, affectionately called Hotel Holly, which was run by a down-on-her-luck lady of the old Newport variety in her family's Gilded Age house. All details there were overseen by her amazing housekeeper, Svetlana, who would be able to converse with Dmitri in his native tongue, if she deigned to converse with him at all. Sveta didn't approve of anyone. She was much harder to please than Holly.

Lilly was leaving for Long Island in three days, on the same day Dmitri and Priscilla were to arrive. It worked out with only one trip to the airport.

Topsy had made a statement to the press saying that she was not taking sides in the divorce and would not be spending any part of the summer with either of her parents. She said she would be working on her dissertation in New York, hoping it sounded like she was the only sensible one of the family and managing to come off as both smug and callous.

On the Russian language front, even though Charlotte and Lilly had had a ten-day intensive in Palm Beach, Kay had managed to keep up. Charlotte, though distracted by divorce and Xanax, was making discernible progress, and now with Lilly off to Sag Harbor, and Kay so focused on linguistic progress, Nina decided to give it up. Lilly had taught her the art of embroidery, and she was interested in making scenes to be hung on the wall. She didn't have the talent or dexterity of Lilly, but she had perseverance, a natural color sense and plenty of time. She hoped maybe this Zen-like activity would have a healing effect on her heart. She thought of Adam as she stitched, and the pain receded slowly week-by-week as did the expectation of a call or an email. I'm numbing up nicely, she thought.

CHAPTER THIRTEEN

The fog had burned off by the time the Russian lesson was over for the day, and Charlotte was stretched out on a soft sofa facing the fire in Seventh Heaven's pine paneled library. She was dozing when Priscilla came in talking a mile a minute, jolting her awake.

"Mrs. D., I printed out your manuscript. I'm impressed. Two hundred and twenty pages, double-spaced. If you'd like, I'll do a line edit for you." Priscilla was eager to get started.

"No, dearie, let me take a look first. Why don't you go into town and get some supplies? Gani doesn't have your flair for the fabulous."

"I'm not going to be part of triglyceride boosting. If you want candy, you're going to have to put on a wig and sunglasses and go buy it yourself."

"Come on, Priscilla. I've halved my sugar consumption, as you very well know, and Gani is very stingy. Only fruit for dessert. And meringues, occasionally meringues."

Gani, immaculate in his white jacket, stood in the doorway and overheard this. "Madame, how can you say that? There are meringues and lace cookies non-stop, every meal."

"I really need some Devil Dogs or Swiss Rolls. Or, better yet, you can get Whoopie Pies here. They sell homemade ones at the gas station."

"Then go get them yourself. I'm not participating in this." Priscilla flounced off towards the kitchen. Her office was in what was formerly called the servants' hall.

Charlotte called after Priscilla. "Buzz kill." She was disappointed but knew Priscilla was right.

Gani followed Priscilla back to her office. "I can make a flourless chocolate cake and put egg white icing on it. That's sort of like a Whoopie Pie, and it won't have chemicals or preservatives or gluten."

"Oh, Gani, what *are* we going to do with her? She *likes* chemicals and preservatives and trans fats and food dye and every other poisonous thing. But go ahead and make this cake. Might as well give it a try."

Charlotte went out to the pool and installed herself on a double chaise longue, which had an awning attached. She made sure she was shaded before starting the edit. Three hours later she found Priscilla in her office and putting the manuscript on the desk said, "It needs some work, but it's better than I thought it would be. I think we can send this part to Tandem Hall and get their feedback."

"Great. I'll put in your corrections, email it and send them a hard copy as well."

"I'd like you to do that line edit first. If you find anything, show it to me before you make the final corrections."

"I don't think I can read it all tonight."

"Take your time. No rush."

Gani went to the supermarket to buy chocolate for the cake and saw the tabloids while in the checkout line. The front pages were full of Colin and Jasmine screaming at each other. He bought two and read them in the car in the parking lot, disposing of them before going back to Seventh Heaven.

He read that the couple was coming unglued. It was reported that Colin said Jasmine was cheating the IRS and that Jasmine said Colin had bankrupted Charlotte on purpose. One of the papers said she was pregnant; the other said he had penile dysfunction. Both had wonderful photographs of radioactive fury. In one she was scratching at his eyes, in the other, it appeared that she was biting his cheek while flailing her arms and kicking his shin. No wonder Mrs. Darling doesn't want to go out, Gani thought, delighting in Colin's karmic kick back.

That night they had dinner on the wide front porch facing Buzzards Bay. Though it wasn't yet dark, Gani had lit candles, which flickered though there was scarcely a breath of air. Even so, Charlotte had on a ten-ply cashmere sweater.

"Dmitri, tell us about Holly," Charlotte said.

"She's an elegant and intelligent woman, as I'm sure you know, and has a wicked sense of humor, but that Sveta must've been a commander in the KGB."

"I've heard she can be fierce."

"Don't believe that gross understatement for a minute. Fierce doesn't even come close."

"I would've thought you could charm her in her own language." Charlotte was enjoying his feigned indignation.

"I could, of course," said Dmitri, tucking into the roast Long Island duckling.

"But?" Charlotte was enjoying herself.

"But I'm more interested in teaching you to speak Russian and hearing about Lilly's defection."

"I'm defecting, too, Dmitri," Nina chimed in.

"My Nina, don't do this to your Dmitri."

"I'll always be your Nina, but I'm not going to Russia, and I don't want to hold Charlotte and Kay back."

They all tried to cajole Nina into changing her mind, but she was adamant.

Kay and Charlotte had been speaking fractured Russian during dinner, but when dessert came Charlotte dropped it entirely and said, "This is the best thing I have ever tasted in all my born days. I'm going to put this recipe in my memoir as my favorite dessert. What do you say to that, Priscilla?"

"I'd say it's a healthy choice. We could even use it for that book *Vain Fare* is doing. I'll ask Gani to make sure the recipe serves eight. That's what they want."

"What shall we call it?" Charlotte liked to name things.

"What about 'Compromise Cake'?" Priscilla suggested.

"Or 'Gani's Gourmet Glory'?" Kay put her two cents in.

"Or 'Charlotte's Confection'?" Dmitri offered.

"Let Gani decide," Charlotte said.

He liked 'Compromise Cake' and said he would work on an icing that used liquid stevia instead of simple syrup so that it could fit in with the theme of *Menus from the Thin and Famous.*

"Okay, Gani, but don't give me the stevia one by mistake."

Priscilla said good night right after dinner. She couldn't wait to start the memoir.

Gani stopped her on the stairs saying, "Have you seen the tabloids?"

"I read them all on the plane and so did Dmitri."

"I wouldn't like for Madame to see them. Very good thing she doesn't leave the house."

"You never know with her. She might enjoy them. Terrible pictures of Jasmine. I had half a mind to bring them, but I didn't because her mother would have a fit."

"What would her mother have a fit about?" It was Charlotte.

"The tabloids, Mrs. D. You would love them." Priscilla said.

"Race to CVS before they close and buy them all for me. You're right. Mom would have a fit. She has always disapproved of them. Smuggle them up to me as fast as you can."

By the time Priscilla got back, Charlotte had showered and was in bed wearing her pajamas with the computer on her lap. "Oh, boy! Close the door and come here." Charlotte stretched her hands out and grabbed the papers.

She flipped through, lingering on the photos of Colin and Jasmine. "These pictures are priceless. I love each and every one. Thank God you managed to get to CVS in time. You've made my day. From now on, make sure if there is anything at all about this cute couple in the press, you'll get the paper straight to me."

"You're so easily pleased. They make the cut most weeks, Mrs. D. If I'd only known, I could've made many of your days."

"Try to get the ones I missed out on. Now, go to bed Priscilla and leave me with these treasures. I'm going read every single solitary word tonight."

Priscilla was equally interested in reading Charlotte's manuscript. She was fascinated by the stories of Charlotte's life but was surprised at how many typos had been overlooked. Charlotte was a very smart and educated woman. How could she not have noticed all these mistakes even with spell check? It was the pills. She knew it, but didn't want to know.

She couldn't put it down and read through the night. The next morning she showed the annotated manuscript to Charlotte. "It's fantastic. You have a gift for the gab, all right."

Charlotte glanced through the corrections. "And you are a wiz at editing. Don't let Tandem steal you away from me."

"Never. Life would be too dull without you. I'll get this in the mail to them today."

Priscilla also tried getting the back issues of the tabloids without contacting the papers directly but that wasn't possible. She decided it was too chancy to call them. If they found out Charlotte was collecting the articles, it would be like waving a red flag at a bull. Charlotte could Google and see what she missed. So far, Charlotte had managed to keep her dignity, and everyone wanted to continue in that vein. So Priscilla just brought the papers as they came out, and Charlotte started following Colin and Jasmine with great interest.

It was unusually hot that summer, and the Sotheby's Real Estate agent was constantly bringing people to look at the house. It was so disruptive for Charlotte's exercise routine, Russian lessons, and memoir writing that by mid-July Kay insisted she take the house off the market for the duration of the summer.

"If Colin makes trouble about this, then so be it, but Charlotte, you can't be kicked out of your own house every day. You need to focus. You can't afford these constant interruptions."

"Especially since there aren't any offers on the property. Only gawkers," Charlotte agreed.

"Mario made this house so pretty, people come here just to take pictures. At least in Palm Beach they have more restraint," Kay said.

"Maybe too much restraint. They don't even come to see the house."

Charlotte made sure there was always someone else around whenever Dmitri was nearby. She didn't know why he made her nervous and started to wonder about her sexuality, or lack thereof. Did he remind her of someone in the past or was she attracted to him? She even considered seeing a shrink when she got back to New York. She thought maybe she should remember whatever there was to remember, that is if there were something to remember. But then this line of thinking made her nervous, and she dropped the idea.

In previous summers Charlotte had chartered the Windward, a 42' Hinckley sailboat. Colin was a good sailor, and she'd enjoyed getting out on the water. It was one of the few things they'd liked to do as a family, and she'd always felt safe with Colin at the helm. Last year, though, a summer storm had kicked up suddenly, and if Topsy hadn't been there to help . . . well, she shuddered to think. Colin had taught Topsy how to sail, and between the two of them, they got back to the mooring in one piece, but barely.

Charlotte had been thinking that not having the boat this summer was the only economy she didn't mind making, and when Dmitri asked them all to join him for a sail, she almost said no. Charlotte and Nina drove down to the marina the next afternoon, and imagine their surprise when they walked onto the dock and found that he'd charted the Windward for August. Dmitri was standing at the stern.

"What a day for sailing, and you won't believe this, but we know this boat very well," Charlotte said as he handed her onto the deck.

Dmitri smiled broadly. "Sailing was my first love. When I was a child, my grandfather lived on a boat about this size in Antibes, a charming town in the South of France. I spent the summer months with him. So I am truly an old salt."

He handled the Windward with easy expertise. Charlotte was able to relax and enjoy the sounds of the sails and the waves lapping the hull. She loved the smell of the sea and the view of Newport from the ocean. She fell asleep and awoke to find the day at an end. "Please invite us again. I want to stay awake for all this heavenly beauty."

"Any afternoon, *Myska*."

There it was again. Too much tenderness. She stiffened and pulled her yellow slicker tighter and linked her arm with Nina's. Then feeling ungracious, she said, "Please, please, Dmitri, join us for dinner tonight. We have much more fun when you're with us."

The next week, Priscilla came into Charlotte's bedroom while she was stretching at the barre. "Your editor called and said to tell you he's very impressed. He thinks you've hit exactly the right note for the memoir. And as soon as you get back to New York, he wants you to meet with their marketing and publicity people."

"This is so exciting! I've been lazy since we got here. Now I'm psyched and will write every afternoon from now on."

That afternoon she took her laptop to the shady side of the deep porch, lit a cigarette and then settled down to write about her high school years. As she reread it, she couldn't help but think, my God, I worked hard. She rewarded herself with an extra half a Xanax and floated through the evening.

Nina left for Sag Harbor the next day and stayed a week with Lilly. Although they never mentioned Adam or George, their absences were palpable.

Charlotte buckled down and demonstrated her world-renowned self-discipline. Not only did she write three hours everyday, but she also managed to halve her sugar consumption again with only a slight increase in Cheetos.

There were several more sails on the Windward with Nina or Kay always in attendance, at Charlotte's request; then suddenly summer was over. The evening air had taken a chill and the days were growing short.

Lilly came to Newport for Labor Day and went back to the city with the others.

CHAPTER FOURTEEN

Energy in New York is in high gear during September. The exhilaration of reentry is what Charlotte looked forward to every year. Rehearsal studios were vibrant with dancers, and this year, her prospective coach, Gail Kirk, wanted to see her at the studio right away to decide if they wanted to work together.

Russian lessons were cut back to the original breakfast hour as the fall routine had started in earnest. Charlotte was always on time for Peter Miller's class, which started at 10. As soon as that ended, she had Pilates, followed by physical therapy. She took her lunch with her and ate in the lounge. The lunches were fuel, plain and simple, and consisted of what she considered pure protein. And on some days that was cold filet of beef, with a side of Béarnaise sauce, some days deviled eggs and some days peanut butter and jelly sandwiches. Gani had to intuit her mood.

The first week back, Charlotte called her literary agent and made a date to meet at Tandem Hall for a strategy meeting and was glad she'd been able to nearly double the size of her manuscript during the summer. She set out on foot to the sleek office on Sixth Avenue arriving precisely on time. Not going to her ballet class felt like playing hooky.

Walking home, she chatted on her cell to Lilly. "You would've been proud of me. I asked for half the advance now. It'll hit my account Monday morning."

"Thank God, we can exhale a little, and I'm not going to take my percentage from this. Just want you to know."

"Thanks, Lil. I'll make it up to you when things normalize. The other half comes when I turn in the completed manuscript."

"Do you want to take the houses off the market?"

"Not yet. Austerity has left me traumatized. I want to build up capital and selling one or both houses would do the trick. I still have to pay off Colin and the lawyers. Anyway, I can always rent."

"Any other news?"

"They like *Charlotte's Dance* for the title. The publisher and the editor were at the meeting as well as publicity and marketing. It was thrilling. They said I can wind it up, and they're sending someone from Tandem to the apartment to go over the photographs with Priscilla."

"I'll help with that. I have some ideas for the cover, too, and a list of suggestions for who could write blurbs."

"I have the rewrite to do, and the editor said the part about breaking my shoulder needs to be beefed-up."

"What does he mean by that?"

"I just wrote what happened without much of the aftermath. You read it."

"Well, as I recall, you were in dress rehearsal for *Sleeping Beauty*, and Colin came in and distracted you mid-leap. Then there you were in your gorgeous tutu, broken on the floor. Isn't that dramatic enough for them?"

"They want more about the paramedics in the auditorium and the reaction of the audience. They want me to describe what I felt in the ambulance and what it was like arriving at the hospital in costume and full stage makeup. That sort of thing."

"If you need any help with the technical vocabulary, I'm sure George Ellis would help you."

"That's okay. I don't need any help. Oh, look. Here I am at Barney's. I'm going in and browse around. See you later." Charlotte tossed the phone in her bag.

Lilly was looking for an excuse to see George and was annoyed at herself for not having had the courage to ask Charlotte to sign the release form he'd given her months ago. Kay had sensed Lilly had fallen for him and was ready to push this along.

Nina was looking for reasons not to return to Middleburg. Kay knew Nina had to get back there as soon as possible and decided to play a role in this, as well. She was never averse to a little matchmaking.

That evening she went to Charlotte's room while she was at the barre and said, "There are a few things that you and I need to do to produce more love in the world."

"Yes, Mother. What do you want me to endorse?"

"No endorsements, just invitations. I think you have to throw a small dinner party and invite George Ellis and seat him next to Lilly. And then you have to think of some reason to get Adam Holt to New York. I have thought of nothing else for a week and can't think of a single excuse to get him here."

"Well, I know just the thing. One of the best tailors on Savile Row is coming to New York for two weeks. They're known for making hunting clothes. Adam can afford the prices, and I bet he could use a new pink coat. I'll call him and tell him he can stay here."

"That might be going too far. Nina would have a meltdown. Just call and tell him about the tailor coming from London and tell him you're having a dinner party. Invite him the same night as George."

"I have some book related work to do so I'll call Adam and George, but you have to arrange the rest with Priscilla and Gani. Call Lobel's and see if they can promise us enough grouse for eight people. Gani makes the best bread sauce. And call Mario to see if he can come and ask him to bring a friend, that makes eight."

"Perfect. But isn't grouse too extravagant?" her mother said.

"Half the Tandem advance comes in on Monday."

"Hallelujah!"

Kay was in her element and seamlessly planned the dinner once she'd heard that both men had accepted the invitation. She informed Lilly and Nina, and both of them acted as if it was perfectly normal to be having these men for dinner, never once letting their inner turmoil show.

Meanwhile, Charlotte had heard from another dancer that the well-known Dr. Heath King sometimes took private patients. He had had a successful practice as a psychoanalyst in New York but had moved on to become a professor at Yale University, taking on very few patients. She had a good reference and was able to get an appointment right away. His office was in his penthouse apartment on Beekman Place. The door was opened by a neat housekeeper, dressed in a gray and white uniform. "Right this way, Mrs. Darling," she said and showed Charlotte into a magnificent library. Dr. King rose from behind his desk and offered her his hand.

Some people might have said the walls were white, but anyone who knew anything about paint jobs, knew that many layers of subtly different shades of white went into giving this lacquer so much depth. The ceilings had a bluish cast with a touch of nacre and seemed to float fifteen feet above her head. She noticed the broad teak floorboards were uncovered, the stainless steel bookshelves were heavily burdened and a motif of lotus blossoms was evident.

"Dr. King, thank you for seeing me. I can tell you, I'm surprised to be here. I've never talked about myself to anyone before." Charlotte immediately felt comfortable with this man. Maybe it was his formal dress and manner. Maybe it was the elegance of his apartment, but certainly he had a special air about him. His steel gray hair curled around the nape of his neck, and his Roman nose was prominent without being too large. His tortoise shell glasses suited him perfectly as did his genuine smile.

"Would you be more comfortable seated here across the desk from me or would you like the sofa?"

"I never pass up an opportunity to put my feet up." She slipped off her shoes and lowered her lean body onto the tobacco colored leather.

"Do you have a specific issue you'd like to discuss?"

"I do. I'm ashamed to say, my daughter doesn't like me very much." Charlotte thought this would be a safe starter. So much had been written on the subject of mothers and daughters that even she knew it was a classic.

"This is something very common. I am sure we can resolve it. Is there anything else you'd like to investigate?"

"I think I'm frigid. I can't stand to be touched. I don't even like massage. I can only bear Thai or reflexology. I know this is abnormal, and though I've been writing my memoirs and thinking a lot about my life lately, I have no recollection of any incident which might have provoked this."

"Don't worry about trying to remember, and just tell me a little about yourself."

Two hours later, Charlotte was exhausted but felt she'd made some progress and made an appointment for the following week. Writing the memoir had opened her up, and she was ready for the help Dr. King could give her. This was surely the right moment for her to have psychotherapy.

She was not ready to announce to her little world that she was seeing Dr. King. Maybe someday, but not today. Her hope was to get over resenting Topsy for resenting her and all the attendant guilt from not being a stay-at-home mom and now a bit more guilt had been added around money. As for the other problem, well . . . she didn't like to think about that and didn't want to have any expectations. She couldn't believe she'd been so open with him in the beginning of the session. Now she wished she hadn't mentioned it.

The following week, she breezed right in and headed for the sofa. Before she'd settled herself, Dr. King started with what would become a string of searching questions.

"Does your frigidity extend to not pleasuring yourself?"

"I don't understand."

"Do you masturbate?"

"I'm not comfortable enough with you yet to discuss this."

"Fair enough. When you look at male dancers do you think of them naked?"

"No."

"What about the female ones?"

"I've seen a lot of them almost naked."

"Do you ever think of caressing them?"

"No. Could we move on to Topsy? This is not why I came here."

"Actually it is, but we can wait, as long as you like, Mrs. Darling."

And there ensued a stilted recounting of Topsy's youth.

Charlotte made the next appointment, but in the back of her mind she saw herself canceling it.

CHAPTER FIFTEEN

The day of the dinner party was stormy. Adam's plane was delayed, but he was only a little late. Mario came with his dapper assistant, Eugene Ware, and George Ellis was right on time. Charlotte, usually the gracious hostess, was not herself. The session with Dr. King had thrown her off, and she'd indulged in a little more cough syrup than usual.

Kay and Mario took over. With Mario teasing everyone and with Kay as his perfect straight man, pretty soon everyone was at ease, and the group was in high spirits when they sat down at the beautifully appointed table. Even Charlotte gasped as she came into the dining room. Gani had put pink light bulbs in all the floor lamps and decorated the table with scarlet autumn leaves scattered on a pink cloth. Thirty-inch peach-colored candles towered over the silver candelabra.

She-crab soup was the first course, but before she'd even picked up her spoon, Charlotte fell face down in the soup; the hairpiece, which she wore when she couldn't get to the hairdresser's, fell onto the table from the impact. She regained consciousness immediately and assured George Ellis, who'd jumped to his feet, that she was fine. He insisted that she go straight upstairs to bed. Lilly mopped the soup off of her face with a napkin and pulled her to her feet.

Charlotte clutched the doctor's arm with her left hand and clung to the brass stair rail with her right and managed to climb the twenty-two marble steps. At the top, she walked ahead of George and Lilly bouncing from one wall to the other like a drunken sailor.

"I didn't know Charlotte drank," George whispered to Lilly.

"She doesn't. Is she having a stroke?"

George caught Charlotte as she was crashing into a wall. "It's alright, Charlotte, I'm right here," he said soothingly. "Can you talk?"

"Yes, of course, I can talk," she slurred.

"Squeeze my hand as hard as you can." She had plenty of strength. "Very good. Now we're going to put you to bed."

Kay was right behind them with Charlotte's hairpiece in her hand. Charlotte was in bed, and George assured them it was not a stroke. But he wanted to see her medicine cabinet.

He opened the mirror above her sink and bellowed, "Good God. Where did all this come from?" And then softly, "Kay, could you get some coffee sent up here?"

George sat on the side of Charlotte's bed and said, "You must tell me everything you took and in what quantity. And did you drink any of that cough syrup?"

"I'm perfectly fine. A little sleepy. I'm just going to take a little nap."

"Oh, no you don't. Start talking. What have you taken? There're enough pharmaceuticals behind that mirror to kill a herd of elephants. Have you been mixing benzos with opiates?"

"How would I know? I took a couple Xanax and drank a few ounces of cough syrup. I could feel a sore throat coming on."

"Did you take a Vicodin, too? This is very dangerous. How long has this been going on?"

"I'm tired. Just let me sleep."

"Keep talking. It's lethal to mix these drugs. I hate to see them sitting right next to each other on your shelf. Did you take both?"

"I don't think so."

Kay arrived with the coffee.

George took the cup. "Drink this, and listen to me. You have to come clean and tell me what you take and how often."

"Oh, God. Don't make such a big deal about this. I take a few of Xanax and sometimes a little cough medicine."

"I see from the bottles, you get these things from various sources, and I see a brand new prescription for Oxycontin in there, too, from Dr. Klein for a surgery two years ago. What did you tell him to get that?"

"My shoulder still hurts."

"And cough syrup from all over the world?"

"I collect it. But I don't take it everyday."

"Charlotte, you're out of control. I know you are a public figure and under a lot of pressure, but you have to stop this."

Kay still had the coffee pot in her hand and refilled Charlotte's cup. The caffeine was having a small, but discernible effect.

"I suppose I'm wasting my breath suggesting you go to rehab." George commented.

"George, you know Charlotte can't do that. I'll stay in the room with her and follow your orders to a tee, but no rehab." Kay was firm.

"Anyone downstairs apt to call the papers?" George asked.

"We know everyone well except Mario's assistant, but I'm sure he can be trusted. I'll speak to Mario and make sure he knows this must stay in the 'family'." Kay knew how to take charge.

"Ok." George then turned to Charlotte. "I'm taking all the drugs with me to dispose of them. I'll give you something to get you through withdrawal and then I want to talk to your other doctors. We'll come up with a plan that'll keep you comfortable but safe.

"Lilly, you and Kay go downstairs and join the others. I'm going to stay with the patient until she goes to sleep. Please give me a shopping bag for the drugs. I'll be down shortly."

George arrived in the dining room as the dessert was being served, and Gani said, "Dr. Ellis, I saved the best grouse for you." He had the main course while the others exclaimed over Compromise Cake.

George made it known that Charlotte was coming down with the flu and advised them all to take one thousand milligrams of vitamin C for a couple of days.

Right after coffee was served Mario and Eugene said goodnight. Adam reluctantly made a move to go and then, changing his mind, said, "Nina, how would you like to get a little fresh air?"

It had been a long time since Nina had seen Adam in his "city" clothes. He looked so handsome in the well-cut dark blue suit, the same color as his eyes. It contrasted well with his thick white hair.

"I'd love some air. Let me get a shawl." They looked so right together. Both of them fit for their ages, Adam six inches taller. Nina skipped up the stairs and wrapped herself in ruffled magenta cashmere. The ruffles softened her close-cropped hair and magenta perfectly set off its steel gray color.

Once they had gone, it left only Kay, Lilly and George in the living room. "I want to check on the patient, but if you'll wait for me, Lilly, I'll walk you home," George said softly.

"I'll be here when you come down, but first I want to thank Gani and leave a note for Priscilla."

Kay went with George to Charlotte's room. "How bad is it, George?"

"I've seen worse, but she should be carefully monitored. Addiction could ruin her life. I can tell by the contents of the medicine cabinet that she's been playing one doctor off another, and I'm one of those doctors she's been fooling. I'll make a conference call tomorrow with the others to make sure she won't be able to play this game anymore."

"Should I spend the night in her room?"

"That won't be necessary, but I'll send a tech here in the morning for fasting blood. Be sure she doesn't have anything to eat or drink before that." He pulled out his phone and started texting the order to the service.

"Anything else?" Kay asked.

"I'd like you to bring her to my office after that. No rush. Whenever she's ready, call me and let me know about what time you think you'll arrive. I can't clear the waiting room, so she may want to wear a scarf and sunglasses."

"She has some wigs."

"Fine. Goodnight, and try to get some sleep, Kay. Everything will be all right." George touched her affectionately on the shoulder and took a large tote bag full of pills and cough syrup with him.

Lilly looked lovely standing by the fireplace in the living room when George came down. She had on a cream colored Valentino pants suit, which set off her dark hair and flattered her slender body. He wanted to tell her how beautiful she was but worried it was not the right time or place.

The September air was soft, and they walked the two blocks east to Lilly's apartment in comfortable silence, each thinking their own thoughts.

"Come up for a nightcap, George."

"I'd love to."

"I want to ask you what you think about Charlotte, but after that, let's change the subject."

"Tomorrow, I'll get her to sign that form, and then I'll tell you everything," George said. "Anyway, I'll know more after I've seen the blood work." He put his finger to her lips. "No more talking about Charlotte tonight."

Lilly opened the front door to her apartment, walking in front of George. She looked around as if seeing it through his eyes and saw a very modern, monochromatic space. A large abstract oil painting and several geometric watercolors. Chrome, glass and leather. No curtains. No rug. Precious few objects. It looked masculine and impersonal, except for colorful embroidered cushions gracing the sofa and chairs. She had the fleeting thought of asking Mario to find a nice rug and help her make it more welcoming. She wanted to welcome George into her life.

George closed the door behind him. And pulled her to him. They fell into each other's arms, exploring one another with hungry kisses.

Sometimes things don't work out, and this was one of those times. George was embarrassed and left, even though Lilly encouraged him to stay. He couldn't believe this had happened to him.

CHAPTER SIXTEEN

At six the next morning, Kay woke with a start. Her telephone pinged a second time. She picked it up and saw the message was from Nina before she realized the bed next to her was empty. Her screen displayed: 74 and 77 alive and well. How's Charlotte? N.

Wiping the sleep from her eyes, Kay typed: Everything's okay here. Have fun, you two!

Kay looked in on Charlotte and found her resting peacefully. Back in the guest room, she sat in the window seat and looked down at the sleeping city. A few cars could be seen with their lights on, but most of the buildings were still in darkness. The city that never sleeps doesn't get up very early, she thought, and climbed back into bed snuggling down and thinking how lucky it was that George had been there for dinner last night. She had total confidence in him and thought he was just the right man to care for both her daughters. She squirmed deeper under the covers and thought about her role in Charlotte's recovery. Then she thought about all the love blooming around her. She happily dozed off for another hour.

By the time the tech arrived, Kay was dressed and caffeinated. He was less nervous this time and drew the blood easily as Charlotte was still half asleep. It wasn't until after noon that she was ready to get dressed and go to George's office. Charlotte had baulked at wearing the wig at first. But after seeing a cover story about Colin and Jasmine in one of the papers Priscilla brought, she flew upstairs and came back down with a short straight blond wig with bangs. Almost not recognizable, even by Priscilla, who'd purchased the wig for a party two years ago.

"I think we should walk. The fresh air will do us both good." Kay called George's office and said they would be there in twenty minutes.

Charlotte's head cleared as she walked. The clearer her head got the more she panicked, contemplating a life without chemicals. Calming down a little, she remembered there were eight sixteen-ounce bottles of Hycodan in her locker at Lincoln Center.

Kay went with her into the consulting room, and they sat in comfortable armchairs across from George's desk.

Charlotte started talking right away. "George, you have to understand that I cannot dance without the cough medicine. Codeine alleviates my arthritis."

"You weren't dancing last night."

"All professional athletes have low grade chronic pain, as you very well know, and most deal with it by drinking alcohol. I don't drink, and I need my Hycodan." Eight bottles wouldn't last forever, after all.

George glanced at Kay and said nothing.

"And at the end of the night I need Xanax or if you want to change it to sleeping pills, okay, but I need something. When I'm dancing, I don't leave Lincoln Center until very late and then I have to eat. I wake up early and start all over again. I don't have the luxury of tossing and turning. I *have* to sleep."

"I'm not expecting you to give up everything. But you have to admit, you've been abusing the stuff and mixing benzos and opiates like that is *not* going to happen anymore."

"You mean I can't have both."

"Right."

"I take a little sip of the syrup every time I go on stage. I honestly need it. For the arthritis, and it helps open up my lungs. And I need the Xanax, too."

"No, you don't. I know your pain has to be treated, and I've talked to all the New York doctors listed on the pill bottles so they're alerted that there was an incident last night. And I've put myself down as the doctor in charge so they will check with me if a prescription needs to be added. I don't like this any more than you do, but what I saw last night was alarming. This cannot happen again."

"Well, if you're not giving me sleeping pills or Xanax, I'm going to need a slug of syrup before bed."

"Sorry, maybe I wasn't clear. You can't have either. I'm going to give you a prescription for fifteen tablets of Percodan. Come back to me when this runs out and we'll reassess the situation. Try to make it last two weeks."

Charlotte did not think she was in a position to argue or negotiate. She would have to make other arrangements, and she would be more careful from now on. She wondered how last night's incident happened. She'd only had the slightest bit more than normal.

Mother and daughter walked home arm in arm. "Your party was a great success, even without you. I think the Middleburg lovebirds are back together, and I noticed George walked Lilly home. She'll never tell me what happened, but she might tell you."

"And you want me to betray her confidence to you?"

"Of course. That's what mothers are for—to know it all."

"Oh, Mom, you're incorrigible. I've got to go back to Lincoln Center right away." Charlotte was anxious to check on her supply of Hycodan. "Please ask Priscilla to fill this prescription at Clyde's for me. I have a costume fitting this afternoon."

"Sure, as long as you promise me to do exactly what George says."

"I want you to know how sorry I am about last night. Will you talk to Adam and Mario and Eugene and tell them I was coming down with something."

"George told them that last night."

"Good old George."

"Mario sent you a nosegay of violets this morning with a card saying he's hoping you kept all the flu bugs for yourself."

"Good old Mario."

Charlotte left her mother at the Park Avenue entrance and the doorman hailed a taxi for her.

She went straight to her locker and put one of the bottles of Hycodan in her purse wrapped in a leotard. Seven bottles left. She then went to the physiotherapist who was practically a member of the ballet company.

"Bob, I need a referral from you. My shoulder has been bothering me lately, and my surgeon has retired. I need something for the pain. Who do you recommend?"

"Dr. Clovis. He has a pain management clinic two blocks from here." Bob wrote out the contact information and gave it to Charlotte.

Charlotte walked there and found that her name got her an appointment and a prescription right away. For thirty Percodans. She was beginning to breathe easier once she'd gotten the pills from a nearby pharmacy.

Once on the street, she called Dr. King. "I hate to call last minute like this, but as I told you, I have all the aches and pains that come with my profession and though, I've never taken any pain meds, I am very uncomfortable now and am hoping you could suggest something for me. Nothing strong as I have to be super alert. I'm being coached for *Giselle*. It's a new ballet for me, and I have to concentrate."

"I can't write a prescription for you. I'm a psychoanalyst, not a psychiatrist. I'm sorry. Don't you have a GP?"

"I did for many years, but he has retired, and I really need something for the pain."

"I can refer you to Dr. Cortez, whose office is on the ground floor of my building. I can call him on the other line and see if he can see you this afternoon, if that's convenient."

"Please call him."

Dr. Cortez could see her, and she got into a taxi and went across town to Beekman Place. Once with the doctor, she started coughing and gasping. "Oh my God, when it rains it pours. I would so appreciate something for this terrible cough. Hycodan seems to work very well for me. I can't afford to get sick now."

This was the first visit to Dr. Cortez, and he wanted to make his famous patient comfortable. He wrote the prescription for the cough syrup and said, "I think Darvocet will do the trick for the pain. Come back later in the week, and let me know if this works for you."

"Actually, I hope you can give me some sort of light sleeping pill as well. I'm in rehearsal now, and I really need my sleep. I can't leave Lincoln Center until late, and I start early in the morning. If you know of something that would give me some rest without making me tired the next day, I would appreciate that as well."

She left with scripts for fifteen Darvocet, ten Ambien and eight ounces of Hycodan. She went to the pharmacy around the corner and paid cash. Finally she relaxed. There were several bottles of Xanax in various traveling cases, which had not been confiscated, and with today's haul, it would see her through until she could figure out how to get more.

She took a little swig of the cough syrup in the taxi going home to celebrate and a Percodan as soon as she arrived. Heaven. And she felt energetic. Why hadn't she known about this before?

The next morning she took two Percodan and raced through her day in a highly functional way. She was jubilant.

Kay said, "You see, Charlotte, you didn't need all those pills and cough medicine anyway. You're much happier without it."

"Yes, Mom." This was going to work out very well.

Charlotte asked another one of the principal dancers who she used as a rheumatologist, and taking that number, called Dr. Jackson for an appointment. Again her fame came to her rescue, and she was able to have another appointment and prescription the same day. More Percodan.

It was important for her to stock up before performances of *The Nutcracker* started as after that, it would be harder to take the time to doctor shop. She would be performing *The Nutcracker*, rehearsing *The Fairy's Kiss* and being coached for *Giselle* as well as taking Peter Miller's ballet class every morning, Pilates class with a personal trainer and of course her Russian lessons with Dmitri. Her beloved dancing now was becoming a chore. Good thing these Percodans revved her up.

Dr. Jackson and Dr. Clovis both wanted her to have an MRI. She would do that right away. They would see how much pain she really could be in. But all this took time, and she had to hide this time from Priscilla, Kay and Lilly. Difficult, but not impossible. She considered fessing up to her sessions with Dr. King. She would tell the family it was the divorce. And it was sort of about the divorce, of course.

Thank goodness she knew *The Nutcracker* so well she really didn't have to rehearse much. Until November she could concentrate on gathering medicines, having MRIs, and generally ricocheting from doctor to doctor. She would make sure the MRIs were at different hospitals and she would show up on time and pay cash for everything.

She needed enough pills to get to Moscow. She remembered that Russian cough syrup was sensational, and there was easy access to Valium, which was her favorite last time she was in Russia. Now, it had suddenly become Percodan.

That evening, she was at home in time for dinner with Kay and Nina. Adam came, too, and the four of them dined in the yellow breakfast room. Percodan brought euphoria to the table, and Kay murmured to Nina, "I can't remember when I've seen Charlotte this happy and full of energy. I think all that Xanax depressed her. Good thing she had that little episode, and George straightened her out."

"Yes, isn't George wonderful? He's out with Lilly tonight." Nina commented.

"Look at you and Lilly! Love is in the air," Kay laughed.

"You and Charlotte better watch out. They say it's contagious."

CHAPTER SEVENTEEN

That weekend, Adam took Nina to see *Hamilton* as well as the famous tailor from London. On Sunday night they dined in Charlotte's yellow breakfast room with the Darlings, who were gratified to see their old friends so clearly in love.

"Whatever you have to do to see *Hamilton,* do it. I don't know when I've enjoyed myself more." Nina was animated. "And Charlotte, you should never have told Adam about that tailor. He's going to be so grand now the rest of the hunt will be put to shame." It was evident from her manner that nothing was too splendid for Adam, and the tailor was lucky to have a famous equestrian like him as a client.

"I happened to have had a photo of Nina riding sidesaddle on me to show the tailor, and he was so impressed, I had to promise to send him a copy to hang in his shop on Savile Row. Now you can count an international model among your friends." Adam was bursting with pride.

"And Adam insisted on ordering a new habit for me. I suppose he did this in case Lola comes back to Middleburg, I won't have to hang my head in ignominy next to her."

"She's nothing compared to you." Adam touched Nina's hand and said to the others, "Anybody who rides like Nina should have nothing but the very best."

"We agree." Kay was so happy with the way things had turned out. Seeing them together, it was obvious the time they'd spent apart made them see that loving and being loved was the high calling.

* * *

By Tuesday it was time for Adam and Nina to go back to Middleburg and try life together. They would live at Beech Hill, though Nina's stable would continue to be run as a business with no changes in personnel.

Kay was helping Nina pack her things in the guestroom. "Kay, whether or not this works out with Adam and me, I want you to know, Covert is your home for the rest of your life."

"Oh, Nina, I'm going to need a handkerchief."

"Pull yourself together, now. Neither one of us is any good at emotion. And like I told Topsy, Covert will go in my will to her and Lilly, but not until both of us have gone to greener pastures."

"You told this to *Topsy*?"

"Why, yes."

"When?"

"When she needed the tuition and so forth to finish her dissertation. It wasn't very much." Nina zipped her carry-on.

"She's such a liar. Let's just hope she has some talent as a writer, and I wish you'd consulted me first. And what's this about a will?"

"Now, Kay, I know how you love to control every single little thing in this wide world, but you can't do anything about our eventual exit from the planet."

"I know. But leaving Covert to Lilly and Topsy?"

"Who else do I have?"

"Well, there's Adam."

"Adam's too old and too rich to discuss."

"I wonder why Topsy never told me you were financing her."

"I told her not to. I wish you would leave that poor child alone. Genetically, she never had a chance. She's secretive like her mother, and she's as stubborn as a damn mule, thanks to you. I like the girl. And so does Lilly. You've got to stop hoping she'll turn into a prima ballerina. Because she won't."

"Why, Nina, whatever are you talking about? I adore Topsy."

"Come on, Kay. You're talking to me. And you're okay with me just how you are. You're an amazing woman but not much of a grandmother."

"Lucky for Topsy, you're my best friend."

"Lucky for me, too. Now, I don't want to spend any more time fussing with you. I want to go back to Middleburg with Adam. My Adam."

"I'm so happy for you both."

"Me, too. I feel very young and foolish."

Charlotte was pleased with herself. Her finances were in order, and she'd started paying Topsy's expenses again. By mid-November, she'd had the two MRIs. Both doctors were sympathetic to her cause after seeing multiple stress fractures to her metatarsals, fibulas and tibias. Most athletes become inured to this sort of chronic pain, but the MRI results were sufficient to justify the doctors increasing the strength of her pain medication. Charlotte was thrilled.

The only hitch was a lot of cash going out the window. Priscilla had never questioned her on cash withdrawals before and neither had the bookkeeper. But if they'd asked, she would've told them part of the truth, that she'd decided to see a shrink and didn't want her family to know. Good thing Tandem had kicked in, she thought. This cash would have stood out a month ago. In March she'd be in Moscow, she kept telling herself, and since she had the opiate flow under control now, she settled into her demanding routine.

Right after Thanksgiving, she was asked to give a formal dinner party for the French Ambassador, and his wife who would be visiting New

York. The Ambassador, Gaspard de Moret, was the brother of Charles de Moret, the man who'd launched Prima, which was still the world's most popular perfume. Over the years Charlotte had become friends with Charles but had never met Gaspard or his wife Alix.

A list of guests had been sent to her from the French Consulate in New York, and her table was filled with people she didn't know but the Consul thought the Ambassador needed to meet. Knowing she wouldn't be able to invite her mother, Lilly, Mario or any of her familiars put her on edge, and it was gratifying to have a sufficient supply of mood enhancers.

Making the apartment look its best for this occasion, Ronaldo Maia used all white flowers and one of the Venetian tablecloths. This one, a rich cream linen with pale variegated ivy tendrils embroidered in the center. The cantaloupe-colored dining room was enchanting with crystal vases in all sizes filled with white blooms of every variety. Upon entering the room, Alix de Moret exclaimed, "Nothing in Paris is prettier. This room is a dream."

At the end of the evening, the Morets agreed the dinner had been a great success, but while walking back to the French Consulate, Alix remarked to her husband, "I think Charlotte must be ill. She looked like she was about to fall over with fatigue when we left, and it's only 10:30."

"Maybe she tired herself out at the matinee today. Didn't you think the venison was delicious? And I loved the chestnut puree." Gaspard tucked his chin into his cashmere muffler and thrust his hands deeper into his pockets.

"Everything was just right. But something's wrong," Alix mused as they approached Fifth Avenue. Bitter winds had plucked the last leaves from the trees lining the sidewalk, and leaden clouds obscured the moon.

"Nothing's wrong, *cherie*. Americans tend to go too fast, do too much, tiring themselves out like children."

"It's more than that. I have half a mind to call Charles."

"What's he going to do? Fly over here and take her temperature?"

She laughed at the idea, and all thoughts of Charlotte were forgotten when they joined the Consul for a nightcap. A lively discussion ensued covering the endlessly fascinating challenges faced by foreign diplomats in the USA.

As she was brushing her teeth, Charlotte thought back over the evening with pride but had to admit it'd been a mistake to raid her hoard of Xanax before the party. She was disappointed with her old love. She definitely preferred Percodan now and wished she'd taken it instead.

Charles de Moret called from Paris the next day. "Bonjour, Charlotte *cherie*. Thanks for entertaining my brother and sister-in-law so royally last night, but that's not why I called. I have good news."

"*Très bien*. I could use some."

"Don't worry about the tabloids. It just makes you more famous. And we want to do another perfume. We are thinking of names now. Pas de Deux. Arabesque. Pirouette. Tutu? What appeals to you?

"What tabloids? I love Tutu. And Arabesque. But Tutu has my vote."

"Maybe we'll do two. You're all over the press here."

"Me or Colin?"

"The text is about Colin and Jasmine, with plenty of pictures of them, but there are also marvelous photos of you dancing at the Garnier and other shots of you when you were in Paris last time."

"I can't believe people are so interested in this."

"You've captured the hearts of the public. We, your French fans, are all sorry to hear you'll be losing your house in Newport, but glad you're keeping Palm Beach. None of us can believe that Colin could like that disgraceful Jasmine after glorious you."

"This summer I started following them on Facebook. Fascinating, like looking at a snake."

"Divorce is distressing, as I know from calamitous personal experience, but it's very good for sales. Sephora can hardly keep Prima in stock."

"That's excellent news, indeed!"

"We'll need new photos. Are you coming this way, by any chance?"

"I'm going to dance with the Bolshoi from mid-March through the first week in April."

"We'll send a photographer to Moscow. The Kremlin would be a great background for you in your tutu. Can you stop here on your way home? We could get some April in Paris shots. Another potential name for a perfume. What do you think?"

"Yes to both. And I would love to stop in Paris on the way back to New York. I'll be traveling with Mom, Lilly and Priscilla for sure and maybe Gail Kirk. She'll be with us in Moscow but will probably have to get back to the States."

"The more the merrier."

"Can you arrange for all of us to be treated like queens?"

"Of course, *cherie*. I love you and your entourage. Maybe I can get to Moscow and see you dance."

"I hope so. You've made my day, Charles."

"We'll put you up in the Plaza Athénée, and photograph you doing all manner of April in Paris activities."

"Wonderful! Like what?"

"Oh, I don't know. Wafting around Bagatelle with spring flowers. Biking across the beautiful bridges with flowers in your basket. Sipping hot chocolate at La Durée with fresh flowers for a tablecloth. And anything else you might like to do."

"I'm going to dedicate the rest of my day to thinking of nothing but you and perfume publicity shots."

"Charlotte, you're not just a star. You're the whole galaxy."

"And I send you love in every language."

That afternoon an outrageously enormous bouquet arrived at 740 Park from Charles as well as a more conventional one from Gaspard and Alix.

Charlotte pirouetted into Priscilla's office. "Dearie, do you think you can rent a rehearsal studio for me in Palm Beach? I spoke to Gail Kirk, and she wouldn't mind leaving the New York winter for a couple of weeks in January after *Nutcracker* is over. We would need someplace for two consecutive hours every day, but we are totally flexible with time. Early, late, different hours from day to day—it doesn't matter."

"La Barre has a great studio on Main Street. Not sure they'll rent it out, but I'll call them and let you know later today."

"If that works out, get reservations for Gani, Gail, you, me, Mom and Lilly on the 10th of January. Coming back here on the 25th. And please tell Dmitri, no hard feelings, but I need a break from Russian lessons while I'm down there. Also, call Sotheby's and say no showings for the house then."

"I'll get right on it. But you have a houseful, and I can work better from here."

"Do you have any M&Ms?"

"Here you go." Priscilla handed her a tiny bag.

"What? Is this left over from Halloween?" Charlotte asked as she tilted her head back and emptied the contents down her throat and then held out her hand for another bag while still crunching.

CHAPTER EIGHTEEN

Lilly sat in her living room and looked around. The rug Mario had sent over went a long way towards taking the hard edge off the room. She would keep it, but she wanted more and couldn't think what that would be. Cream-colored curtains would be perfect but impractical considering New York City soot.

A Christmas tree, she thought, would do the trick. She pulled on her short down jacket and headed for Second Avenue. Once the tree was up and tiny white lights were plugged in, she realized she had no ornaments, having always spent Christmas at Charlotte's. Never mind, she thought, and picked up the phone to call George's cell.

The call went to voicemail. She hung up, and paced the room, eventually calling George again.

"George, I'm glad I caught you! I put up my tree and hope you'll come over this evening to toast it with me." How lame I am was her only thought.

"I would love to, but today I have a parents' thing at the girls' school, and we leave to go skiing on Saturday morning. I'm a full-time father until after the first of the year."

"Have the best vacation ever and give me a call when you get back." Lilly hoped he didn't hear the catch in her voice.

"Will do. Merry Christmas and Happy New Year to all of you!"

Lilly sat down and tried to be a grown-up but found she couldn't and let the sobs rack her thin torso. This is ridiculous, she told herself, and cried on.

By the time Lilly woke up, it was dark and the only light in her apartment was from the tree. She checked the time. Five-fifteen. She picked up the phone again and called Charlotte.

"Don't bother asking George to Christmas dinner. He's taking his daughters out West to go skiing."

"That's funny. I was just at his office to pick up my prescription, and he said he was taking them to Vermont."

Lilly sighed, "I guess I got it wrong." So very wrong.

"Why don't you come over here? Nina and Adam are arriving in time for supper. Mom was just about to call you. I've got to dance but will come back here right afterwards."

"I'm on my way over now."

Even Charlotte, who never noticed anything, noted how miserable her sister sounded. She'd also discerned a deep sadness in George.

Charlotte had enough sensitivity to hate herself for being sort of pleased that this romance seemed to be over. She would talk to Dr. King about that. Why was she so mean-spirited lately? She certainly didn't want George for herself and didn't require Lilly's undivided attention. But in her heart, she didn't want them back together. She struggled with these feelings and decided to take the high road if it ever presented itself to her.

By the time Charlotte returned from Lincoln Center her library was filled with laughter. Nina and Adam had brought a lot of joy with them and their happiness had spilled over and dispelled Lilly's gloom.

"Charlotte! I'm so glad you're home. I can finally make my toast!" Adam moved quickly to the bar and poured Charlotte a flute of chilled Champagne.

"Ladies, please raise your glasses with me to drink to the health of my darling Nina who has put me on cloud nine by promising to be my wife!"

"To Nina," they all cried out in delight.

"Okay, Adam, I'm ready to show off the ring now."

Adam took the pouch out of his pocket and proudly slipped the ruby onto the fourth finger of Nina's left hand.

Christmas was perfect as usual, thanks to Priscilla, Gani, Ronaldo Mia, the singing Santa and Kay. Mario stepped easily into Colin's role as host and kept everyone, even Lilly, laughing.

The happiness of the season had a softening effect on Charlotte, and on December 26th as she was on her way to dance *The Nutcracker* matinee, she said, "Mom, I know it's none of our business, but things seem to have simmered down with George and Lilly. I wonder if you have any dynamite you can use to fire that up."

"You know Lilly hates us to even be aware of, much less talk about, her off-campus activities. I'd say leave it alone. You see him often. Why don't you invite him for dinner and see what happens?"

"I'll do what I can," she said, knowing she wouldn't. The high road was too lofty after all.

Meanwhile Nina and Lilly went for a walk and a talk in Central Park. "I was so sorry George didn't join us for Christmas. I hope you're still seeing him. He seems like such a nice man."

"He *is* a nice man, but he doesn't seem interested in pursuing me, and I've never been one to chase a guy."

"Maybe there's been a misunderstanding."

"I don't think so. We had a brief almost-affair. Twice we tried to consummate our attraction for each other, and it didn't work either time. No one is at fault, but now we're both embarrassed."

"Lilly, don't let a little sexual malfunction stop your relationship. Things can change as you get to know each other better. I think you jumped into bed too soon."

"I'd be happy to keep seeing him, but when I asked him over for a drink, he said he couldn't and right away told me he was taking his daughters skiing for Christmas as if he wanted to preempt my inviting him to Charlotte's."

"I wouldn't give up so easily. Adam and I had a misunderstanding that might've finished us off, but he took a chance and came to New York at Charlotte's suggestion—to buy more hunting clothes of all ridiculous things. But, as you see, it worked."

"Do you have any suggestions?"

"Let me think about it. Actually, it's your mother who has the conniving mind. Don't worry, we'll figure this thing out."

Nina walked back to 71st Street with Lilly and went up to see Kay. They could see the tree twinkling from where they sat in the library having ginger tea. "I tell you, Kay, you have the two most wonderful daughters. I feel as if they are part mine."

"Because, of course, they are."

"For twenty years I've celebrated Christmas in this apartment with you and the girls, and each one was special, but this was the best of all. Everything was perfect and, imagine, I'm getting married!"

"I should be in the fortune-telling business. Don't forget, I was the first one to see this coming down the pike."

"True, and now you need to think of how to put Lilly and George back together."

"I talked to Charlotte about that today. She's going to give a dinner party and invite George."

"That's a terrible idea. Charlotte is flat out and will never be able to do that until after Moscow. Something needs to be done soon."

"Like what?"

"I don't know. You're better at this than I am." They discussed possibilities for half an hour, and then Nina got up and said, "I've got to get back to Adam. I left him at the Carlyle with all the newspapers spread around him and the TV blaring. We're having dinner with his cousins, the Snowdens, tonight. I've got to make myself presentable."

Nina had her wedding to plan and Adam's family to meet, and Kay had Charlotte to manage. Somehow nothing ever got organized for Lilly and George.

Sensing nothing was going to happen, Lilly said to Nina, "I need a break. I know this is a terrible time to leave Charlotte, but Mom's here, so I would love to go back to Middleburg with you and stay at Covert for a couple of weeks."

"That would be grand. I'm living at Beech Hill, but I didn't drain the pipes at Covert, and Howard can go over and crank up the heat. We're on Delta leaving Thursday morning. All your things are still in your old room waiting for you. It's been too long, Lil."

"I know. I can hardly wait to get there."

"We can ride every day and hunt three times a week. It'll be like old times."

"I can't think of anything better."

"Why don't you invite Topsy down?"

"What a good idea. It'll do her a world of good. She acts so tough, but she isn't really."

"I know. And Covert is her home, too. I'm leaving it to the two of you in my will."

"Don't ever talk about dying, Nina. You're more my mother than Mom in all the ways that count."

Lilly got Topsy on the phone. "Oh, Aunt Lilly, I'd love to go." Her voice was full of enthusiasm. "All my best memories are there, and I need to fan them for my novel."

"Good. Tell me a little about your book."

"I'm writing for the pre-teen reader, and it's about a girl who loves to ride and lives—guess where—Middleburg."

"Is it a mystery? I remember how much I liked Nancy Drew when I was a kid."

"Sort of. I was telling Adam about it at Christmas dinner. He says it sounds like his kind of book, and he's seventy-seven, so maybe it has a broader audience. He's so cool, marrying Nina and all."

"I'm delighted for them both."

"Mom says they've known each other, like for*ever.*"

"They both grew up in Middleburg, so of course they have, and it sounds like that's just the place for you to write. Come to me for breakfast at eight on Thursday, and we'll go to the airport together. I'll get your ticket."

"Thanks, Aunt Lilly."

"I'm staying for two weeks, but Nina said for you to stay as long as you like."

"I might take her up on that. There is nothing here for me."

"Topsy, how can you say that? You're twenty-seven. New York is a fabulous place for someone your age and all your school friends are here."

"I'm so over those girls. I'm not like them. They're so phony and all over me because of Mom. They just want to see her dance."

"Be fair, Topsy. Most people do."

"Whatever. Anyway, I haven't left the city in a long time. I'm psyched. I'll be at your place right on time. And I'd love an open-ended ticket."

Lilly put down her needlework and thought about Topsy for a moment after the call ended. It was true that she stood in her mother's shadow, but then so did most of the world. Lilly herself was so inured to the shadow that she'd rarely even felt the chill.

As soon as they arrived at Covert, Lilly and Topsy changed into jeans and made a beeline for the stables. They both loved the horsey smell and breathed in the air with joy, like welcoming an old friend. There was one new groom, but they knew everyone else and were happy to find they could take two horses out for the afternoon. They were expected for dinner at Beech Hill, but not until seven.

There were patches of snow on the fields and the ground was hard. Neither of them had been on a horse in over a year and wanted to spend a couple of hours riding, no matter how saddle sore they'd be tomorrow. It was beginning to get dark when they brought the horses back and lights were on in the tack room. And there was Nina, her face pinched in distress.

"I would have come after you, but I didn't know what trail you'd taken. Adam had another heart attack. Ben Toler says he'll be fine. It was a mild attack, but he has to stay in the hospital for a few nights. I'm so glad you girls are here, and I'm going to stay at Covert with you until Adam comes home."

"We're so sorry. What can we do?" Lilly put her arm around Nina's shoulders and held her close.

"Nothing, really. Howard's going to bring the food over, and we'll eat at home. I'm going back to the hospital now and again after dinner. But don't worry about me. Howard will drive."

CHAPTER NINETEEN

Adam was still in the hospital on New Year's Eve. He was looking marginally better, but he was in the right place. Nina, Lilly and Topsy took dinner and silly hats with them and stayed until the end of visiting hours. Once back at Covert, they turned out all the lights, lit some candles and sat in front of the fire in the living room, chatting until well past two.

Charlotte was dancing that night and went out afterwards with some of the other dancers. Unfortunately, she had some Champagne, which didn't mix well with the pills, and left incoherent messages on many phones.

The next morning in Middleburg, messages were compared, and Lilly lost the straw draw and was the one to call Kay. "Mom, Charlotte was drunk last night."

"Don't be so silly. Charlotte doesn't drink."

"You should have heard the message on my voicemail."

"It may have been a bad connection."

"Nina and Topsy got similar messages. Slurred and nonsensical."

"Now, Lilly, it was New Year's Eve, and she went out after the performance with some friends. I certainly wouldn't worry about her drinking."

"I'm not really, but I *am* worried that she's abusing pills again."

"How can she be? George only gives her two week's supply at a time. She never asks for more. She is exceptionally highly disciplined, as you very well know."

Lilly sighed and wished her mother a Happy New Year and turned to face the others. "Mom only sees what she wants to see." She remembered Charlotte saying exactly the same thing to her not so long ago.

"Let's go out and gather the morning's glory before it's too late." Nina led the way to the stables. Lilly and Topsy followed, stiff and bow-legged, still sore from the first ride.

Howard made sure they ate black-eyed peas and collard greens for health and prosperity in time-honored Virginia fashion. Later Nina took the good luck meal to Adam and stayed with him the rest of the day.

For her part, Charlotte was hazy about what had happened the night before. When her mother asked about the voicemails, she couldn't imagine what she might have said and laughed it off. With the help from a couple of chemicals, she felt no worse for wear and rushed to Lincoln Center for another *Nutcracker* performance. She didn't have time to worry about it. Kay went with her and took over. Kay liked to worry.

Talking to some of Charlotte's friends, Kay found they'd gone clubbing, and no one said they'd noticed anything amiss. That was enough for Kay to calm down and assure herself that Lilly was overreacting, as she thought Lilly often did. Nothing niggled in the back of her mind.

Dmitri had had too much vodka on New Year's Eve to be able to cope with much of anything the following day and couldn't play his voicemail until January 2nd. When he arrived at Charlotte's for the breakfast lesson, he said, "*Myshka*! How thrilling to have a midnight call from you!"

Kay sat up and listened attentively.

"At midnight I speak better Russian than I do in the morning." Charlotte wondered what on earth she'd said.

"I think you are a very naughty *myshka*. My favorite kind. And where did you learn such terrible words?"

"Those weren't terrible words. Just a terrible accent."

Dmitri arched his eyebrow, made a kiss with his mouth and handed Kay and Charlotte pages titled, "Muscle Verbs".

"Now, class, I think you're ready for a field trip, and I'm inviting you to Skovorodka in Brighton Beach for dinner and then on for dancing."

"Was that where you used to go with Misha to get stuffed mushrooms for Balanchine when he was in the hospital?"

"How did you know this?" Dmitri straightened his back and looked serious.

"I came to New York with some other dancers from Washington in December of 1982."

"And you've waited all this time to tell your Dmitri?" He shook his finger at Charlotte.

"I was so young and unmemorable. I didn't want to mention it."

"I'm going to call Misha and tell him you remember us. He will be so pleased."

"I was starstruck by Misha, of course. Give him my love and tell him when he comes to New York, we'll have a party. Mario is always talking about the roast suckling pig at the Breslin. You have to be a group of eight to order it. If he'd like that, I'll host everyone there."

"I hope that includes me," said Kay.

"Of course. The three of us, Lilly and Mario plus three more." Charlotte made the calculation on her fingers.

"I'm going to call him right now." Dmitri took out his cell and pressed the number. Baryshnikov's voicemail took the message, "Charlotte and I are longing to see you, my friend. Hurry to New York." Before the message ended, the return call came and after a spate of rapid Russian, Dmitri asked Charlotte, "When do you return from Florida?"

"January 25th."

He turned back to the phone and said in English, "Excellent. We'll see you in February.

"Now, ladies, settle down to these verbs, and I'll plan our field trip when Misha is here. Even though Lilly's Russian is not as good as yours, I think we can include her. What do you think?"

"She missed most of the summer lessons, but she made a big effort to catch up. I bet she can read the menu and order," Kay said.

"I was just teasing. Of course she will come with us." Dmitri laughed his big laugh and handed them another sheet of paper, "Hyperactive Adverbs".

Adam got out of the hospital but was forbidden to hunt until further notice. "Look, Nina, let's go somewhere warm. If I can't hunt, I might as well be a no-account lay-about lazing in the sun."

"We can go to Palm Beach. In fact, I would love to have our wedding in Charlotte's garden, if that's okay with her. Just the family. And there's a wonderful minister down there, Jim Brown. I'd like him to marry us. We can go now with the others, make the plans and get married in April, when Charlotte's back from Moscow."

"Okay, if that's what you want. But I don't want to be the only man in a house full of women. Let's stay somewhere else."

"The Colony is just two blocks from Charlotte's."

"That's too close. Let's stay at The Breakers. We can play golf. I'm pretty sure that tyrant Ben Toler doesn't have anything against golf."

The Palm Beach weather was perfect. Gail coached Charlotte two hours a day at La Barre studio. They walked on the beach in the early mornings and had dinner on the terrace most nights. Nina and Adam joined them one night at City Diner in West Palm Beach. Kay knew Adam would love the meatloaf, and Charlotte loved to go there. Huge bowls of bubble gum flanked the cash register. Charlotte rarely allowed herself wads of gum, but she figured dining at the diner was a legitimate exception for the no chewing gum in public suggestion made by PR.

They sat in a red leather booth with electric trains circling the ceiling moldings, listening to a 50s jukebox.

Nina asked Charlotte, "What's the name of my favorite shop in Palm Beach? The one that wraps everything so beautifully? And has those fabulous shocking pink bags?"

"Mildred Hoit."

"I know they have all sorts of wonderful things, but do they have wedding dresses?"

"I think it's more casual, but they have trunk shows all the time. It's worth a try. You can walk there from the Breakers."

"Adam, let's go tomorrow."

"Nina! What do you mean, 'Adam, let's go tomorrow.'? It is, 'Kay, let's go tomorrow.' The groom can't see the wedding dress until the wedding day. Everybody knows that." Kay was emphatic.

Nina and Kay went off to Mildred Hoit's the following morning and chose an ice blue silk dress with an off-the-shoulder portrait collar. It was the color of Nina's eyes and flattering to her steel gray hair.

That night, Charlotte and Gail went to the Kravis Center to see the Miami City Ballet and, later in the week, to Alvin Ailey. Between the two of them they knew quite a few of the dancers, and both nights they went to Buccan after the show for a drink. Other than that, it was early to bed for Gail, Charlotte and Kay.

* * *

Topsy had stayed in Virginia to ride and write, and she often rode with Julia Wilke, assistant manager of Nina's stables. At a loss for evening entertainment, the two young women planned to see *Hamlet* at the Folger, an Elizabethan-style theater in the Folger Shakespeare Library in nearby Washington.

Topsy and Julia were both five-eight with lean, muscular physiques. Topsy with her long honey-colored hair and big hazel eyes and Julia with her short black hair and squinty pale blue ones turned a lot of heads walking into the Folger, including Sabrina's.

Sabrina Rolland was a part-time house manager, whose duties included meeting and greeting people at the theater. The other part of her time was taken up by culinary classes. She was training to become a pastry chef at L'Academie de Cuisine.

Sabrina tripped over herself trying to get to them so she could show them to their seats, but the crowd was too thick, and she only made it to the door in time to see them settling into the plush red seats near the center aisle, five or six rows back from the stage. It was not every night that Sabrina spotted anyone of her own age. She was from the Eastern Shore of Maryland and even though she'd moved to Washington ten months previously, she hadn't made many friends.

Accepting that she was now officially lonely, her New Year's resolution had been to introduce herself to every young person she saw at the Folger. So far she'd met no one, but the year was young, and she was determined.

At the intermission, Sabrina stationed herself at the door and waited for Topsy and Julia to come out, but they didn't. Shoring up her resolution, she went right down the aisle and leaned over and said, "Welcome to the Folger. This is your lucky day, and I am inviting you both for pizza after the show."

Julia was quick to reply. "It *is* a lucky day, but we've already eaten. Maybe we could have coffee with you after the play."

"How about the Starbucks next door?"

"We'll see you there," Julia said.

Once Sabrina was out of earshot, Topsy grabbed Julia's arm. "Are you crazy? I don't want to hang out with a total stranger."

"I have to have some coffee to make the drive home. My sister would give anything to work here. Maybe this girl can get her an interview."

"Let's not make it long. I need to get back to my book."

"One cappuccino. Promise."

In the car going back to Middleburg, Julia said to Topsy, "I can't believe you invited Sabrina to come for a ride. You know nothing about her equestrian skills, and I don't want any of my horses harmed."

"Come on, Julia. That poor girl is so lonely. If she calls, we can spend an afternoon with her."

"She'll call all right. I never saw any eyes light up more than hers when you mentioned horses. You can't be having strangers at Covert."

"You're the one who agreed to coffee."

"There's a big difference. You invited her home."

"She probably won't call."

"Of course she will, and then she'll fall off the horse and sue us."

"Relax, Julia. She's probably a great rider. She's from the Eastern Shore, after all. Just think of all the possibilities. She could get your sister a job at the Folger, become your new best friend, and don't forget all the pastries."

Sabrina called the next day and made arrangements to come on Saturday morning. She arrived with smart jodhpurs on and handled the horse with skill. After the ride, Julia had to stay at the stable to teach a dressage class, and Topsy took Sabrina to the Red Fox Tavern for lunch. It was nearly three before Sabrina got in her blue Prius for the drive back to Washington. The plan was that she would return at eleven the next morning.

CHAPTER TWENTY

Charlotte and Colin's divorce was final on January 27th. It was 10:30 when Kay got the call from the lawyer. Charlotte was in Peter Miller's class at Lincoln Center. Kay got right into a taxi and was standing outside the studio when Charlotte came out.

"Mom! What a pleasant surprise. What brings you here?"

They were alone in the lounge when Kay broke the news. Charlotte shed a few sentimental tears but quickly pulled herself together. "Look, Mom, I have to carry on with the day, but I can be home by six. Can you make sure we have dinner alone with Lilly? Just the three of us?"

As soon as her mother had left the room, Charlotte called Priscilla. "The divorce is final. Ask Gani to make his chicken curry with papadums. And lots of Compromise Cake. Remember, chocolate is medicinal, so please leave a care package in my room with whatever you've got."

"Don't worry. I'll take care of everything. If there is anything else, just let me know."

"I couldn't do without you, Priscilla."

"I couldn't do without you, either."

"Is there anything I should know?"

"Charles de Moret called from Paris. Everything is shaping up for your visit. He's coming to Moscow for your final performance and is working on having the company jet from Moscow to Paris, and he sends you his love."

"Charles is the best. Anything else?"

"The writer from *Vain Fare* would like your favorite recipes. I'm sending the recipes from the luncheon he attended and the cake, of course. Do you want to add something?"

"I can't think about it now. I'm going to skip Peter's class tomorrow so we can talk then."

This was unprecedented, and Priscilla worried that Charlotte wasn't as detached about the divorce as she appeared.

Charlotte hesitated for a moment and then continued, "Help me think if there is anything I need from Seventh Heaven. I can't make it to Newport before leaving for Moscow, and Colin may sell it before I get back."

"I had all your clothes sent here after Labor Day. Topsy has some things there, but not much. Your mother and Nina cleared everything out of the pool house."

"It's no longer my house as of today. But my lawyer said I could go back and take any personal things. After twenty-two summers, the whole place is a personal thing. Especially the garden. That garden was a precious gift to me wrapped up in honeysuckle and roses."

The melancholy in her voice sent a shaft of compassion through Priscilla. "Next summer, you can come to Maine and stay with my parents. You'd love it."

"You're so sweet."

"Beware of paparazzi today. I'm sure Jasmine will make the most of this as interest in her has been waning lately."

"I'll check out Facebook and Twitter. I'm a big fan of Jasmine's. She certainly knows how to handle the press. Don't forget to get any interesting papers."

Charlotte swallowed hard and prepared to meet the press. She promised herself to bone up on post-marital etiquette and keep everything civilized.

She went to her locker and had a big slug of Hycodan. Only three bottles left, damn. She then straightened her back and consciously lowered her shoulders before opening the door onto West 65th Street.

There was a small group of photographers waiting for her as she left the rehearsal studio. She waved to them and then joined them to answer a few questions. Putting on a big smile, she said she wished Jasmine and Colin the very best. She mentioned she was focused on training for dancing *Giselle* with the Bolshoi and launching a new perfume in Paris.

"What will you do in the summers, now that you have lost Newport?" one of them asked.

"I'm thinking about going to France," she said without thinking. Then reflected, what a good idea.

The next week the tabloids came out with pictures of Jasmine at Seventh Heaven. Despite the February temperatures she was scantily clad, even on the porch.

"You've got to hand it to this woman," Charlotte said to Priscilla as they were pouring over the papers in Priscilla's office. "Listen to this. She's having the garden readied for a *Landscape Digest* shoot in June, and *House Sensational* is planning a ten page spread for the June issue."

"Colin couldn't have owned the house for more than an hour when these photos were taken. There's no dust on her."

"Somehow a shingle cottage in New England doesn't suit her. I'm sure it'll be on the market soon," Charlotte mused.

"Do you want it back?"

"Can't afford it. Anyway, I've been thinking I might like to rent something in France. Something near Paris. Wouldn't that be fun?"

"Count me in."

"Get Alix de Moret on the phone for me. She'll know how to go about this."

After speaking to Alix, Charlotte called Lilly. "Now hear this! I've just made arrangements for renting Gaspard and Alix's Paris apartment and their *manoir* in Normandy for July and August. They're going to the Cape and were delighted to rent it to us so their staff will have something to keep them busy."

"So the price was right?"

"Both places for less than renting in Newport. I'm so excited!"

"I hope there's room for me."

"The Paris apartment has four bedrooms, and the manor house in Normandy has ten."

"Oh, my God. We're going to have so much fun! Where's the apartment in Paris?"

"In the seventh. Rue de Varenne. Right across from the Rodin Museum."

"Have you told Mom?"

"She's next on my list. Priscilla says she's in. And Gani and Cookie can have a well-deserved two months off. I'm going to give them tickets to the Philippines."

"Is there a pool in Normandy?"

"No pool, but there's an equestrian center five minutes away."

"Perfect."

Early the next morning, Charlotte was at George Ellis's office checking in and getting her allowance of Percodan.

"Charlotte, a friend of mine has offered me four tickets for the Cirque du Soleil. I would love to invite you, your mother and Lilly."

"How lovely! When?"

"Almost anytime as my benefactor works for the company."

"In that case, I accept and will get back to you as soon as we three girls can get our heads together and pick a date. Would next week be too early?"

"Name the day."

On her way to Lincoln Center, she called Priscilla and asked her to find a date when all three could go and email George Ellis with the information. The last thing she wanted to do was go to the Cirque du Soleil, but she thought she could always produce some sort of excuse at the last minute. She'd never liked the circus. It didn't make any sense, but it had been like that since she was a little girl.

Priscilla made the arrangements for the following week, and that evening Kay said to Charlotte, "What's this about the Cirque du Soleil? I can't believe you want to go."

"I'm not going to go. But you're so set on getting Lilly and George together, I thought I'd better jump at the opportunity."

"And let a ticket go to waste?"

"It won't go to waste. Someone will have a wonderful last minute surprise."

"And me? Am I supposed to be the third wheel?"

"You're the matchmaker, Mom. You figure it out."

"I don't want to go either. Trapeze acts always give me the heebie-jeebies. Think I can just tell George the truth?"

"No."

"Too awkward? He wants a chaperone?"

"Call Nina. She'll tell you what to do."

Kay got Nina on the phone first thing the next morning. Nina listened carefully and said, "Kay, George wants to see Lilly, not you or Charlotte, but he is doing this in his own way. You can close your eyes during the high wire parts and tell Priscilla she will have to fill in at the last minute for Charlotte."

"Now we have to get Priscilla involved in this, too."

"Yes. So the two of you can leave George and Lilly at the end. If you're there alone, they would have to deal with you, and they shouldn't have to deal with you."

"I don't know how Adam can stand you, Nina. I hope you don't boss him around the way you do me."

"I treat Adam like a king, but trust me, you need Priscilla for your exit plan."

"Is Topsy still in Middleburg? Is she driving you crazy with suggestions on how to run your stables, your house, your life? She's just like you in the bossy department."

"She's helping me with wedding plans. It is all set for May 8th. Charlotte will be back in plenty of time. It's going to be in the gazebo at noon and a family luncheon. Nothing formal."

"So how's Topsy helping? Sounds like there's nothing to it."

"I hate to order things online, and she's doing all of that and writing her book and riding with me. Some friend of hers from Washington comes out here and rides with her and Julia on the weekends."

"Who's that?"

"Sabrina Somebody. Nice young girl. Cheerful. Very good for Topsy. She's smiling a lot more."

"Well, that's at least something. Don't let her start giving you her opinion on every last thing."

"I'm fond of Topsy, and she doesn't bother me one bit. Adam's still under doctor's orders to take it easy. I'm glad to have her company."

"Wish you'd come to New York."

"I'm too happy here. What about you? Why don't you come to Middleburg?"

"And have to conjure up excuses for why not to ride in the sleet and snow and freezing rain like you two nutcases? No, thank you. Anyway, a lot's going on here. The divorce settlement is captivating the press, and there are my Russian lessons. I don't want to get behind. And Baryshnikov is coming soon. We're going to have dinner with him. He's an old friend of Dmitri's."

"Middleburg can't compete with that."

"I know."

CHAPTER TWENTY-ONE

Lilly and George hardly noticed Priscilla had replaced Charlotte for the Cirque du Soleil. The initial awkwardness between them melted quickly as the amazing performance spread its magic through the audience, but Priscilla was aware of Kay's tension. "Mrs. Darling, do you want to leave? I'll take you home if you want to go."

"Maybe at the intermission. I don't know why this is so stressful for me."

"Just close your eyes."

During intermission, they migrated to the lobby. George went to get drinks for them, and Kay said to Lilly, "I want the three of you to stay, but I have a bit of a headache and want to go home."

"You don't have a headache, Mom. You just hate to watch acrobats, and Charlotte inherited this from you. I knew she wouldn't be coming tonight, and I'm surprised you made it this long."

"I didn't know you knew this about me. I always took you to the circus when you were little."

"You were hyperventilating most of the time. I'll get an Uber and wait outside with you. Priscilla, tell George I'll be right back."

"Mrs. Darling, I'd be happy to go home with you."

"No, dear, you stay for the show," Kay said.

Kay made her getaway, and George commented, "I hope it wasn't the music that gave her the headache."

"Everything's perfect. She's just run down and needs to take better care of herself."

As soon as the performance was over Priscilla made her excuses. George took Lilly's arm and they huddled together in the frosty night air walking eastward. George said, "Why don't we go to the King Cole Bar? They have just the sort of food I'm in the mood for."

"Good idea. Let's walk." Lilly looked up at George. He leaned down and kissed her lightly on the lips.

Luckily the corner banquette was available, and they enjoyed a panoramic view of the room with the famous Maxfield Parrish mural.

After ordering Champagne and Lobster Thermidor, they giddily discussed the possibility of spending a romantic winter weekend in New England.

"I know just the place in the Berkshires, and I can assure you of sleigh rides in the snow."

"Can you arrange for hot chocolate with whipped cream afterwards?" Lilly teased.

"I can, and I solemnly promise everything will be to your liking."

Personal performance angst aside, the evening was a huge success.

Remembering the expense of three hundred pounds of Valentine hearts Charlotte had sent to her colleagues last year, Priscilla took the bull by the horns.

"I found Giant Hershey's Kisses online and have ordered a hundred and fifty of them and will organize wrapping and delivery, if you'll sign these cards." With that she gave Charlotte three bags of fifty cards, the kind that preschoolers give to each other.

"Priscilla, you're so clever! Please order another twenty-five, and I'll give them to the doormen and Dmitri and Mario and Gani and, and, and. . . ."

Charlotte enlisted Kay to help her sign each card with x's and o's and question marks.

Misha's trip to New York coincided with Valentine's Day, and those chosen for the field trip to Brighton Beach met at Charlotte's for a glass of vodka and a bite of Beluga. Baryshnikov, though retired, retained every inch of his regal posture. Still handsome and fit and so elegantly dressed, he brought a magnetic force with him wherever he went.

Charlotte, despite her own fame, was in awe of him. Every move he made was perfect, every word he uttered, charming. Kay was blushing like a schoolgirl, and Gani came in with paper and pen asking for an autograph. Lilly was quiet, but happiness, having nothing to do with Misha, seeped out of her every pore.

After the vodka, they Ubered over to Brighton Beach. Lilly did not understand much of the conversation, which was conducted in Russian, but a smile never left her face. After dinner Misha and Dmitri invited the Darlings to a club. Lilly said she couldn't join them, hopped into a cab and rushed to George's apartment on Central Park West.

The next morning Misha attended Russian breakfast at Charlotte's. "Look at your magnificent birds! Canaries sing such thrilling love songs."

"Sometimes I wonder if it is right to have them in a cage like this, but they would never survive in New York, even in summer."

"And you have given them such a marvelous Victorian cage. I'm sure they like the yellow curtains and the generous supply of tulips. Where would they find a better setting for themselves?"

"Misha, you always know what to say."

The class that morning consisted only of Charlotte and Kay, and they discussed what a good time they'd had the evening before, using muscle verbs and interesting adjectives. A beaming Lilly arrived as Misha and

Dmitri were leaving. She greeted them and made her excuses in very respectable Russian.

When Charlotte got home from Lincoln Center there was a note from Priscilla saying that the editor at Tandem had called and asked for an additional chapter. He wanted her to write about the divorce.

At first Charlotte was furious, but as it was after business hours, she slept on it and called the next day. "I'm not anxious to discuss the divorce, and I'm well aware that the details as reported by Jasmine and Colin have been spread all over the tabloids and social media. So there's not much that the world doesn't know."

"It's time for your side of the story to come out. People can't get enough of this. It'll boost sales enormously," he promised.

"To be honest with you, my mother handled the whole thing for me. I was under a lot of pressure to perform and really stayed removed from the whole divorce, getting the juicy bits from the same sources as everyone else."

"Write about that. You've been silent on this subject all along, and people want to know why. Say you couldn't bear the psychological anxiety. Say you needed your mother. Your fans will eat it up."

"It happens to be true."

"Even better."

It was quiet in Middleburg. Adam was recovering, and Topsy was getting on with her book. And, Julia and Topsy were getting to know Sabrina Rolland.

One morning out riding with Nina, Topsy said, "Look, Aunt Nina, Sabrina just knows me as Topsy Stone. She has no idea who my mother is."

"Uh huh."

"Let me tell you, it's a relief to have a friend who doesn't want to talk about Mom all the whole time. I don't think I've ever known anyone who didn't know who my mother is. So I'd like to keep it like this."

"I understand. But who your mother is has a lot to do with your life experience so she'll have to find this out if you get to be good friends."

"For now we're just getting to know each other, and I love being anonymous on the Mom front. I put all photos of her in the house away when Sabrina came to visit."

"I'll warn Adam not to say anything, and we look forward to coming for dinner. Have you sampled her cooking yet?"

"Julia and I went to her apartment for dinner last week with Julia's sister. She made some fancy salmon thing that was delicious. It was cooked in a puffed pastry. You won't be disappointed, I'm sure."

"Does she want to work in a bakery or a restaurant?"

"She talks about having a B&B on the Eastern Shore. She wants to live in the country."

"Sensible girl."

That Saturday, Sabrina cooked a dinner, which endeared her to Adam. Chicken Pie and Apple Brown Betty with outstanding hard sauce.

Adam called Covert the next morning. Topsy was in the shower, and Sabrina answered the phone.

"My dear Sabrina, you're a genius in the kitchen. It was the best of all possible meals. Just what an old guy like me likes to eat."

"Just what I like, too, Mr. Holt."

"I'm sending someone over with the *New York Times.* Tell Topsy there's an article on her mother in the Arts section that she'll be interested in. Why don't you girls come here around 12:30, we'll have lunch at one."

When Topsy got out of the shower, Sabrina was sitting on her bed with the phone still in her hand. "You didn't tell me you have a mother that they write about in the *New York Times.*"

"Oh, God. Now, you know." The color drained from her face and she looked like she had sustained a physical blow.

It rained hard that day and after what turned out to be a tense lunch, Sabrina and Topsy had planned to spend the afternoon in the kitchen at Covert, Sabrina doing her baking homework and Topsy writing her book.

"So how did that work for you with your mother constantly in the public eye?" Though her back was to Topsy and she seemed to be concentrating on the recipe, her voice was aggressive.

"Usually my aunt Lilly came to parent-teacher things with my dad. But I can remember the teachers asking me if my mother would be coming. Pretending to be concerned for me, but really just wanting to meet Mom." Topsy kept her voice neutral.

"And what about the school play and concerts and things?"

"I have to give Mom her due. She'd come if it were at all possible. And so would Aunt Lilly and Dad. Pepita would always be there, too."

"Who's Pepita?"

"My nanny."

"South American?"

"She was Basque. From the northwest of Spain."

"Was?"

"She died last year in a convent in San Sebastian where her sister was a nun. Mom made sure I got there for the last days of her life and stayed for the funeral. I was mad at her for not going with me, but she was dancing *Firebird* and couldn't really."

"I bet there were a lot of times when she 'couldn't really.'" Sabrina turned and faced Topsy.

For the first time in her life Topsy jumped to Charlotte's defense. "People save their money to see her dance, to be in the room with her and feel her energy. It's not fair for them to have the understudy, is it? Just so I can have my mommy at my side. I'm a grown woman."

"You weren't always a grown woman." A nasty undertone could be detected in Sabrina's voice.

"It's funny, but today I can see she did her best to make sure all the bases were covered. I used to only remember the times I scanned the audience hoping to find her face and not finding it. After a moment of desolation, it made me feel sort of self-righteous in hating her for not being a regular mom. But she never could have been."

"She should have been there for you."

"Maybe I shouldn't have shamed her for not being there, and I never appreciated the others who were always there. Most kids only had their mothers. I had Dad and Pepita every time and usually Aunt Lilly and sometimes Mom and Granny as well."

"So you don't resent your mother, and yet you never mentioned to me who she is?"

"I didn't think it was relevant to going riding with you."

"She's such a big deal."

"Yes, she is. She's an exception to all the rules, and I guess I was glad for someone to like me for me and not for her. Sorry if that bothers you."

"It doesn't bother me. I just think you should've told me." Sabrina's voice was whiny now.

"What? Hello, I'm Topsy Stone, daughter of Charlotte Darling. Is that what you think I should do?"

"Something like that." Sabrina turned back to her dough.

Topsy couldn't wait for Sabrina to leave. She wanted to call her mother and tell her she loved her. No, she wanted to go to New York and tell her in person. What she didn't want to do was to sit here in the kitchen and watch this stranger measure flour and sugar.

"I'm going to get my laptop and come back and write."

"Get the computer and run away from this conversation."

"Whatever."

"Don't you 'whatever' me."

Topsy shrugged and left the room. She took her time and when she returned the whole ground floor smelled of heavenly homemade bread, but Sabrina had packed up her things and was heading out to her car.

"Bye, Sabrina. I'm going back to New York. I'll call you when I get back in the spring." Topsy called after her.

"Whatever."

Sabrina did not look back.

On the drive to Washington, Sabrina berated herself for being so heavy handed. This, she told herself, is why I have no friends. Why can't I let it be what it is? Do I really have to be so critical all the time? At least I can keep in touch with Julia and get her sister an interview at the Folger.

Topsy showed up at Beech Hill at suppertime. Nina saw the lights of her car and flipped the outdoor lights on. "Hello, honey. Where's Sabrina?"

Nina was happy to see Topsy was alone. She hadn't liked Sabrina. She hated to admit that even to herself, especially since there was no particular reason for her not to like the girl.

"She went back to Washington. She's a little too aggressive for my taste." Topsy was matter-of-fact.

"Oh, how's that?"

"She seemed annoyed I hadn't told her about Mom and, like, accused Mom for not being a good mother. What does she know?"

Nina focused all her attention on Topsy. "Come on in. Adam's upstairs. Give me your coat, and we'll sit by the fire."

Topsy followed Nina into the living room. While peeling off her jacket, she said, "Mom did the best she could. She can't act like an everyday mom when she's the most famous dancer in the world. I see what discipline it takes for her. She has never been lazy one day in her entire life."

"I can vouch for that."

"She has always wanted the best for me. How could I have expected her to be normal when she's so abnormal that the whole world acclaims her and wants to watch her dance? I never appreciated this. I expected her to be herself and a different self as well." Topsy was warming to her new insights.

"Humm."

"Sabrina showed me something. No one has ever attacked Mom before in front of me. Now I see a different side. I'm sorry I spent so many years making her feel as guilty as possible. I always thought it was her, but I was the self-centered one. Always crying for the moon." Topsy wailed.

"Topsy, let's find some balance here." Nina put her arm around Topsy's shoulders.

"You don't understand, Aunt Nina. I blamed her for everything and never looked at my part. I've been downright mean to her. And I'm so sorry. I've refused all her efforts to get together, time after time.

"Granny tried to tell me that I was hurting her. She tried to show me how selfish and spoiled I am. And I hated her, too. I hated her for trying to show me my mother is exceptional. Imagine! The whole world knew what I wouldn't see."

"Here have a glass of sherry. You're overwrought, dear." Nina poured a small amount.

Topsy threw the amber liquid down in a single gulp. "I want to go to Moscow with them. Do you think they'll let me go?"

"I don't think that's a good idea. The tension of dancing *Giselle* with the Bolshoi will be extreme. I think you should reconcile on home territory." Nina's brow was furrowed.

"But now that I see how much I've hurt her, I want to be with her all the time."

"Why don't you spend the night here tonight? We can call Granny and your mother in the morning." Topsy's newfound passion was unnerving to Nina. So atypical of the girl.

"But don't you see? I was whining about not having a normal childhood, and it was Mom, darling Mom, who had the really strange one. Imagine having to become a professional at age eight. What was I on about? And Granny! Why did she push her so hard?"

"Your mother was born with an incredible talent. Granny did what she saw as her duty."

"And Aunt Lilly? What about her?"

"I hear Adam coming downstairs. Why don't we discuss this in the morning?" Nina was anxious to turn down the emotional dial.

CHAPTER TWENTY-TWO

Topsy spent the night at Covert but was back at Beech Hill before nine the next morning.

Nina answered the door. "Adam has gone into town to run some errands. Let's have coffee in the kitchen."

"I have these yummy sticky buns that Sabrina left."

"Adam will be thrilled." Nina took the plastic container from Topsy's outstretched hand and carried it into the kitchen.

"I've been thinking, and I think it's all Granny's fault. She wanted Mom to be a star for her own glory, and she's ruined everyone's life."

Nina sat down wearily on the wooden chair. "I'm sorry, Topsy. Which lives are ruined?"

"Well, Mom's and Lilly's and mine."

"Your mother has been so successful that one of the most important publishers in America wants to publish her memoirs, and she is only in her early fifties. This is a sign of great success. She has made millions and millions of dollars. This is another sign of great success. Businesses from all over the world want her endorsement for their products, another sign.

"Lilly has made a fortune and has a very interesting life. You've had the luxury of having had a superior education and extensive world travel as well as a privileged upbringing all because your grandmother dedicated herself to your mother's talent. You have to understand these are not ruined lives. Please go home and grow up."

Topsy turned on her heel and left the room.

Tears of frustration sprang out of Nina's eyes. I'm so angry at them all, she thought. Angry at Topsy for being a twenty-seven year old adolescent. Angry at Charlotte and Lilly for whatever they did or didn't do to allow her turn out like this. Angry at Kay for being right about Topsy. Angry at Adam for being wherever he is and not here with me. And angry at myself for all this anger.... Nina stamped her foot and opened the back door. She breathed in the cold dry air and let herself sob.

Adam was walking in the front door as Topsy was stumbling out. "Hold on, Topsy. What's the matter?"

"Every single goddamned thing."

"Let's go to Middleburg and have a cup of coffee. Just the two of us."

Forty-five minutes later, Topsy had come to the end of her complaints and had begun to hear herself.

Adam patted her on the hand. "I think you see this is not a matter for blaming anyone but really a matter of being appreciative of all the love you've had from so many people. I don't think you would've wanted any other life."

"Oh, Adam, you're the bomb. Thanks for letting me vent. I'm so glad you know all the players in my drama but are enough of an outsider to listen without being personally offended."

"I think Nina's right, though. You need to realize that your grandmother's determination and your mother's discipline have brought a great deal of beauty to this world as well as many benefits to all your lives."

"I'm beginning to know. I'm going to stay here for another few days. I'm going to think about how to make it up to Mom and Granny. Then I'm going to New York and try to be part of my family again."

"I hope you'll come have dinner with us tonight."

"I'll be there at seven."

They bought some flowers for Nina, and Adam drove Topsy back to Beech Hill to get her car. He found Nina sitting quietly by the fire doing some needlework.

"I just had coffee with Topsy."

"Then I guess you know we had a kerfuffle."

"Everything's okay. These flowers are from her."

"Thank God for you, Adam."

He ruffled her hair. "Women," he said.

Topsy took long solitary rides and thought about how she could convince her mother and grandmother that she'd changed. The more she thought the more she remembered incidents, which made her cringe with regret.

Finally, she decided to invite the two of them to her apartment and cook dinner for them. But what did they like to eat? Of course, she knew about her mother's sugar addiction, but other than that, she had no idea.

She Googled around for food ideas from the 60s and 70s and came up with devilled eggs and cheese fondue with the right kind of Coke to start, followed by tuna and broccoli casserole. For dessert she was sure original Klondike bars and Swiss Rolls would be a big hit.

She picked up the phone. "Priscilla, it's Topsy. I want to invite Mom and Granny for a meal. When would that be possible?"

"I'll have to double check, but it looks like you can have any night after the performance this week. Or next Thursday. She's not dancing next Thursday."

"Next Thursday would be great. My place at seven. Let me know. Thanks."

On the day of the dinner, Topsy had pastel-colored helium balloons delivered in the afternoon and brought home an armful of Casa Blanca lilies. She remembered the garden in Newport was full of them. She scoured the city for peonies, but it wasn't possible to find any in February.

As the fragrance of the Casa Blancas filled her small apartment with their heady scent, she remembered being in the garden with her mother when she was very little, shorter even than the lily plant. Topsy could picture her mother photographing her that day and wondered where the photos were.

Topsy's eyes stung. She swallowed back the tears and set the table with things she'd been given by the two guests expected that night. Topsy knew she had to be careful with tears. If she let them out too easily, she would start wallowing in self-pity, but if she cut them off, she risked killing the emotion.

By the time Kay and Charlotte arrived, Topsy had fluffed every cushion and closed the curtains. She hugged and kissed them and told them how much they meant to her and how sorry she was to have been surly for so long. Mother and grandmother were delighted to have been invited to her apartment, though a bit surprised by her unusual warmth and constant flow of compliments.

"Tops, I love what you've done here," Kay said. "I'm glad you've hung these hunting prints. Your grandfather and I bought them for the house in Middleburg when your mother was a little girl. You know, this color reminds me of butter."

"It should. The name on the paint can is Butter Yellow."

"I like this pale blue you've used with the butter," Charlotte observed. "And all these wonderful balloons swaying to a disco beat. With real Coke to boot!"

"These lilies smell like summer in Newport to me." Kay was determined to notice everything, and she didn't fail to praise Topsy for choosing an imaginative menu.

In the taxi going home Kay said to Charlotte, "Kids today take all these effect-specific drugs. Do you suppose there's one for loving the family?"

Charlotte whipped her head around to face Kay. "You don't think she's on Ecstasy do you?"

"I've never seen her like this. The pills are multi-colored with smiley faces on them. So they must make you smiley."

"Mom! How would you know a thing like that?"

"Mainstream media."

"I don't think she's on drugs, but her behavior was totally out of character. And what was with all those balloons?" Charlotte fiddled with her earring.

"I want to put my two cents' worth in. I don't think it's a good idea for her to come to Moscow. Maybe Paris, but only if she continues to be interested in us," Kay said.

"She'll probably drop us like hot potatoes, but I'm glad she's writing her book. And it's nice to know she's been enjoying her time in Middleburg."

"I could've done without the reading. I've never liked listening to authors read their books." Kay searched in her bag for a Kleenex.

"I think it's more that the subject of her book isn't interesting to us. But at least she writes clearly."

"Clearly boring, if you ask me," her grandmother said.

On the first of March, Charlotte rang Priscilla from her bedroom. "Listen, Priscilla, I need you to be very diplomatic and call Tandem and tell them the last chapter can't be turned in before I go to Moscow."

"Don't worry. I don't think they were expecting it so soon."

"That's good because it's not possible to finish it before we leave. After we get back from Paris, the heat will be off. I'll write it then."

"Did you start it?"

"Barely, but don't tell them that. Tell them I want to include the Bolshoi experience in the book."

"Okay. They'll like that."

"And phone Dr. Heath King on Beekman Place and cancel my appointments. Tell him there's been a sudden improvement on the Topsy front, and I'll call him when I get back."

"Right." Priscilla wondered why this name wasn't familiar to her but sensed this was not the time for questions.

"And I want you to be sure you pack enough M&Ms and Marlboros and things. It'll be highly stressful for me in Moscow, and I don't want to have to make do with whatever the Russian versions are. Do you understand how important this is to me?"

"Definitely. Do you want enough American junk to last through Paris, or just for the three weeks in Moscow?"

"I like everything in Paris. I never need to bring supplies there. You know that. I have to get dressed now. Talk to you later."

Charlotte had been short with everyone lately. She was worried she'd need more pills to take to Russia, just in case she couldn't see a doctor right away. The density of the schedule alarmed her. Breathing deeply, she reminded herself dancers worldwide have access to the best doctors.

CHAPTER TWENTY-THREE

Topsy's re-entry into family life had been jerky. Her efforts had not been determined enough to pierce through the tough agenda which was in place for her mother during the final weeks before going to Russia.

Priscilla had plenty on her plate but was pleasantly surprised when Topsy dropped by her office. "I know Mom has already left for Lincoln Center, but I thought I'd just hang out with you and see her when she gets back."

"You might be here quite a while. So make yourself comfortable."

The phone rang constantly. Priscilla had an answer for everyone, but no time to chat. Topsy studied the Moscow schedule. There were ten days of rehearsals before the performances started. Four hours per day were scheduled with the whole Corps de Ballet and an hour alone with Gail Kirk plus a daily hour with Gail and the Bolshoi's retired Giselle. Before and between rehearsals and command performance dinners there would be television and newspaper interviews, practically everyday. There would also be an official ball in St. George's Hall in the Kremlin Palace, two dinners with the Minister of Culture at Café Pushkin, afternoon tea with Putin in his office in the Senate Building and a special guided tour of the Crown Jewels. Even at her age now, Topsy knew this sort of schedule would be a stress test. How did her mother manage?

Topsy's new awakening allowed her to see not having access to Charlotte was not a slight directed at her but rather a result of relentless demands. Sitting there in Priscilla's office gave her a clearer understanding of what was involved with dancing *Giselle* in Moscow.

Boris, Priscilla's designated contact at Aeroflot, was becoming a pain in the ass with his incessant calls wanting to make sure everything was perfect for Charlotte's flight. Aeroflot was providing the entire first class cabin for her use and were bending over backwards to have exactly what she would like to eat and drink. Boris was accustomed to VIP passengers. He understood Beluga and all the top-end Champagnes and vodkas. He was baffled by sugar cane Coke in glass bottles and requests for specific snack items he was unable to get through his usual channels.

"Look, Priscilla, really, egg-shaped Reese's Peanut Butter Cups? Not an easy item to locate. And aren't they the same thing as the round ones?"

"It might be for you and me, but not for Mrs. Darling. She likes the egg-shaped ones, and this is the time of year you can find them. You're just not looking hard enough, Boris."

There was a great bellow on the other end of the phone. "Boris is famous for perfection."

"Relax. Mrs. Darling's very sweet. She'll be thrilled you thought of Klondike bars and Cheetos and Charleston Chews. If you can't track down egg-shaped Reese's, I'll bring some."

"I'll track them down, don't you worry. Now, just to reconfirm, the limousines will arrive at the 71st Street entrance of 740 Park at four p.m. on the 14th. Passengers are Charlotte Darling, Kay Darling, Gail Kirk and Priscilla Odom, is that correct?"

"You know it is. Hang on, Boris. Mrs. Darling's on the other line."

"Priscilla, get Dmitri on the Moscow leg of the trip. I won't be able to manage with only an official translator. I *have* to have Dmitri. I know he has other students, but it's only three weeks. I'm panicking. Convince him."

"Right on it."

Nina switched back to Boris, "There'll probably be another passenger. Dmitri Shumakov. I'll call you back with his passport number et cetera as soon as I can."

Priscilla got Dmitri on the line. "Mrs. D. wants you to come to Moscow. Please don't tell me no. She'll flip out."

"I dream of such an invitation," he said. "Night and day, I dream of it, but I can't."

"What do you mean, 'can't'? This is an emergency."

"I have other responsibilities."

"She says she won't go without you."

"Is this really true?"

"She says she's panicking."

"I'll see what I can do."

"Aeroflot will need your passport number. Do you need a visa?"

"No visa necessary for me, thanks. And I'll call you this afternoon to let you know. I know you're under a lot of pressure, yourself, dear Priscilla. I won't leave you hanging."

"Dmitri, your sainthood is certain."

Just then someone she knew from the *New York Times* called to say 'their man in Moscow' would need an interview, which would be published in the international version as well. "I can call PR and get back to you, or you can call them yourself, Ned."

Once that was settled, Priscilla, turned to Topsy, "Sorry it's so wild here today. Do you want to come back later? I forgot to ask your mother what time she'd be home. I can call her back, if you want."

"Please don't bother her. Granny said I would be welcome to join them in Paris and to tell you my plans. But from what I see here, the Paris schedule is just as packed as the Russian one. I doubt if I could shoehorn in a breakfast date with her."

"You could come to all the events, but it's true, there's no room on the schedule for spontaneous action."

"I was hoping to get to go to Moscow with them. I see they're staying at the romantic Hotel Metropol. But Granny said, 'No way,' to Russia."

"Now you know why."

"How does May look?"

"She'll have to turn in the final chapter of her memoir. The release date is September 14th. Then there's Nina's wedding in Palm Beach on May 8th. I'm sure you'll be there. Quite a few post-Bolshoi interviews. Not much going on in June. She rented the Moret's house in Normandy and apartment in Paris for July and August. I know you'd be welcome there anytime."

"I don't know how she does it all."

"She's a freak of nature."

"Count me in for France. You choose the dates."

"Why don't you come on July 15th and leave August 8th? I'll get your ticket."

"How far is the house in Normandy from Paris?"

"I hear it's hour and a half away, but not at rush hour. And there's a train. I don't have the specifics on that, yet."

As soon as Topsy left, Priscilla called Dr. King, gave him the messages and wondered how long Charlotte had been seeing him. She hoped Charlotte was addressing the pill and sugar situations, although she hadn't noticed any signs of improvement. In fact, she'd noticed glazed eyes and a slip in the usual total attention to every detail. Probably, just focused on the choreography, Priscilla thought. Then she thought, I'm beginning to think like her mother.

The phone rang again. This time it was Dmitri.

"I can come. Will bring my passport with me in the morning."

"I'll have a copy of the schedule for you. We'll have lots of time to ourselves during the rehearsals. I'm counting on you to show me the town."

"I'm from St. Petersburg, but I know my way around Moscow well enough. I will be delighted and honored to be your private guide."

"We may have to let Lilly and Kay tag along."

"Of course, but not everyday."

"My mother wants me to get one of those fur hats for my dad, but I doubt he'd ever wear it."

"Probably not, but we can go to see Elena Yarmak, Moscow's favorite furrier, and have a look."

"I'm so glad you're coming. Bring your tuxedo. I've got to go. Mrs. D. is on the other line."

Priscilla switched phones. "What can I do for you, Mrs. Darling?"

"Try to get Dmitri to come with us to Moscow. I really need him there. You'll have to convince him, though, as he has other pupils."

"You already asked me to see if he could come."

"I did?"

"Yes, and it's all set."

"I'm just confused with all that's going on. Tell him I'm thrilled. Is my mother overseeing the packing?"

"She is, with schedule in hand. You'll have everything you need. You dance and we'll take care of the rest."

"How could I ever manage without you?"

"You couldn't," Priscilla laughed but knew she'd spoken the truth. The thought that perhaps she should mention the memory gaps to Lilly flitted through her mind, but the phone rang another ten times before she left for the day.

A schedule like this suited Charlotte to a tee. She loved not having a moment to think of anything other than music and dance and pills and sugar.

CHAPTER TWENTY-FOUR

Kay had analyzed the schedule and packed three suitcases for Charlotte and then packed two contingency ones as well. Once Dmitri's bag was added, there were twenty-four pieces of luggage, including carry-ons, but Aeroflot was not dismayed and took care of everything for the party of six. It was a great luxury to have the whole cabin to themselves, and Charlotte was duly impressed by the impeccable service and excellent selection of food and beverages.

The Minister of Culture was at the airport in Moscow to meet them accompanied by two legendary tour guides. The Minister was a charming man who spoke flawless English, and Kay and Charlotte traveled with him in a hand-built ZiL limousine. The chauffeur proudly informed them that only a dozen of these cars were produced each year. The traffic was worse than in New York, but they sped to the Metropol in the special ZiL lane reserved for VIPs on official business.

The Minister introduced them to the waiting hotel manager and stayed with them as they were shown their rooms. Despite the long flight, Charlotte maintained her regal posture and was able to express her delight with the Presidential Suite in Russian much to the surprise of the staff.

"I admire this suite, sirs. The painted ceilings are magnificent as are the marvelous antique tables and chairs. The beds look very comfortable and the size of the dining room permits me to entertain. You are too kind and thoughtful. This American ballerina is honored. These rooms are glamorous as for a movie star."

The hotel staff applauded this speech, and Dmitri beamed his approval, as did Kay and Lilly. Priscilla and Gail Kirk took Charlotte's linguistic accomplishments for granted.

Charlotte and Kay's baggage was left in the two-bedroom Presidential Suite, but they continued along the hall to see the junior suites reserved for the others. Charlotte continued to comment and compliment in Russian.

As soon as they got back to their rooms, Charlotte kissed her mother and said she wanted a nap now and would unpack later.

Standing at her bedroom window, gazing through a thin veil of snowflakes at the magnificent facade of the Bolshoi, Charlotte felt a surge of emotion strangely like nostalgia. Suddenly, she longed for Natasha Jitkoff, her mentor from long ago. Natasha had been dead for years. Charlotte had been dancing in London at the time and was unable to attend the funeral.

The physical force of grief swelled from where it had been hiding and smashed her. Her knees buckled, and a strangled cry came from deep inside of her. She held onto the window-ledge to steady herself. Quickly, she stiffened her back. No time for this, she thought, and picked up the phone. She had to push forward.

The hotel doctor arrived right away. Kay heard the doorbell and came out of her room. "Go back to bed, Mom. It's someone from the Bolshoi to welcome me. I've asked for a wake-up call at four so we can have tea together before we unpack."

"What a sensible girl you are. Make this a short visit and get to bed yourself."

Charlotte sat with the hotel doctor in the living room. In Russian she said, "I appreciate your coming right away as I have left my prescription pills in New York."

"Tell me what you need, Mrs. Darling."

"Percodan, for the pain. Cough syrup with codeine to open up my lungs and something light for sleeping."

"I cannot give you something for sleeping as well as Percodan. Surely your doctor in New York doesn't do that."

"You are correct, but as I have no time for a sleepless night in Moscow, I thought a little something would be helpful."

"Why don't you give me the name and number of your physician in New York, and I will discuss it with him."

"I'm jet-lagged and don't think I really need the sleeping medication. So if you would be so kind as to give me a month of Percodan, two a day, and some cough syrup, I'll be fine." Not as easy as she thought.

"I'll have the prescriptions filled and sent up to you immediately." As he left, he bowed formally and brought the back of her right hand up to his lips.

Charlotte waited for the delivery, took it into her room and stood by the window again watching snowflakes skitter across the square chasing each other with wild abandon. Memories swirled through her mind, focusing more and more on Natasha's passion for purity. Standing there, hugging herself for warmth, Charlotte could feel Natasha's disapproval roll towards her across hurdles of time, space and eternity.

The following morning after a welcoming ceremony at the Bolshoi, Charlotte asked to see the company doctor and explained to him that she'd forgotten her Percodan and Ambien. At least he had the courtesy not to ask for contact information on her New York doctor. However, he did warn her that sleeping pills and Percodan don't mix and was stingy with the amount, counting the days out precisely.

The Bolshoi dancers were highly skilled, as she'd expected, and very friendly as well. The former Giselle, whose name was, in fact, Giselle, turned out to be a great beauty in her late thirties. She'd retired recently to marry a high-ranking government official and was now pregnant with her first child. The three women, Giselle, Charlotte and Gail Kirk, the coach from New York, spent their first session together getting to know each other and watching some outstanding clips of the ballet filmed in various locations.

At the end of the day, Charlotte went to the hotel tearoom with Gail. It was a winter garden with a fountain and a large, domed stained-glass ceiling. A harpist was playing softly in one corner. Charlotte turned to Gail. "What did you think of Giselle, the person, not the ballet?"

Gail replied, "I couldn't get a read on her. All business. Very professional."

"Striking, too. She seemed sad, though."

"Everything you'd expect from a prima married to the State."

Charlotte ordered a Coke and lit up a Marlboro. She hoped this Giselle had a soft side and an approachable doctor.

"Did you get a look at the guy dancing Albrecht? His name is Ivan Orlov," asked Charlotte.

"I saw him, and he's definitely a hottie. You've got all the luck, Charlotte."

"All the luck and about twenty more years on this planet than he has. Maybe I could bring him home for Topsy. Have you met Topsy yet, Gail?"

"I haven't. But anyone would be glad to meet Ivan."

"Anyone but Topsy. She's a finicky girl."

Priscilla came in and joined them. She sat down and slipped off her shoes. "I'm about toured-out. But I found out something I think you need to know."

"Do tell. We love to know everything." Charlotte scooted to the edge of her chair.

"I hate to be the one to break this to you, but you can't be the only two in Moscow who don't know." Priscilla hesitated.

"Out with it."

"One of the principal dancers tried to commit suicide when Giselle left the Bolshoi to marry an oligarch."

"Which dancer?"

"Ivan Orlov."

Charlotte and Gail caught each other's eye and fell silent for a moment.

Priscilla continued, "I don't know what part he dances, but I heard he's very handsome. Blonde and blue eyed, looking for all the world like a male version of Giselle. Their love story appeals to the Russian soul, as our guide told us with tears in his eyes. Apparently when they danced together in her last performance, there wasn't a dry eye in the house. Did you meet them?"

"He's my partner in this production, and we were with Giselle today for over an hour."

"How long ago did this happen?" Gail asked.

"Eighteen months."

"I'm so glad you told us, and considering this, it can't be easy for him to have me as Giselle. Did the guide tell you why they parted?"

"A terrible misunderstanding involving another dancer. Or maybe it wasn't a misunderstanding, but it was definitely terrible and involved another dancer. I had trouble following the story. It was told in half Russian—half English. Ask Dmitri. He was practically crying himself."

"Maybe it's best if I pretend not to know about this," Charlotte mused.

"Good idea."

"Don't tell Dmitri that I know. And don't tell Mom and Lilly. The less said, the better."

The next day Charlotte woke up feeling tense. Free-floating anxiety, she diagnosed and prescribed herself an extra Percodan.

During the rehearsal, she paid special attention to Ivan, but he didn't display any signs of depression. Charlotte began to wonder if Priscilla had the story straight. It could have been any one of the other dancers, some of whom seemed positively morose. In fact, Ivan seemed the most cheerful of the lot, and she accepted a dinner invitation from him for that night.

Jetlag felled her, and she had to beg off the dinner plan. The next morning Ivan tapped on her dressing room door. "Come in." Charlotte was seated at the table with a large powder puff in her hand.

"I've got a little something for the jetlag especially for you." He put a small glassine envelope on the table.

She looked down at it and then up to Ivan's face. "I've never tried it."

"Then wait until the end of the day. I'll come here and enjoy this with you."

"All right," she said and ignored the quiver of fear scaling her spine.

Throughout the day, she thought of the glossy little envelope with the white powder and how innocent and pure it looked. As she was being fitted for the last costume, Ivan sent a note saying he was waiting in her dressing room.

When she arrived, he had the lines laid out on the mirrored top of the dressing table.

"We'll do a different dance tonight," he said as he leaned to inhale the first line.

Charlotte was not expecting the instant exultation when the drug hit her brain. "Where has this been all of my life? I'm launched! Let's tear-up the town."

Ivan dropped Charlotte at the Metropol as the sun was painting the Volga a vivid pink.

Kay was pacing the living room floor. "Mom, what are you doing up? Get some sleep!"

"I was just going to say the same to you."

"I've never felt better. I'm going to shower and go to the Bolshoi. I can't wait to get to the barre. I don't feel the least bit tired."

"I'm glad you had some fun last night, but take it easy. You have an official dinner tonight. The Minister of Culture is taking us to Café Pushkin. Private room. Eight-thirty. You need a manicure."

"Only you would worry about that. I'm fine without it." Charlotte brushed past her mother and went to her bedroom and closed the door.

She smiled at her reflection in the mirror and said, "I'll only use this here. Don't worry I won't get hooked. I need this for the run of *Giselle*, and I should enjoy it. Thoroughly enjoy it, the whole time I'm here. Maybe in Paris, too. It'll be fun to do this in Paris. Plenty of time to quit once I'm back in New York. Not going to be a problem. Wahoo!" She did a little jubilation dance. A few steps executed with precision and joy.

Ivan was already stretching at the barre when Charlotte arrived. She kissed him on both cheeks and said, "I feel like I can fly."

"You can and will. Wait until we have the audience. Nothing better than coke enhanced applause."

"I've fallen in love with dance all over again."

"I'll follow you to your dressing room with the supply." Ivan looked furtively over his shoulder.

"I feel so sorry for the others not feeling this elation."

"I have plenty for you and me, but not enough for the whole *corps*."

"Don't get me wrong. I don't want to share. I just wish everyone felt like this."

The day passed in a flurry of activity and excitement. Ivan was included in the Minister's dinner and at the end Charlotte said to Ivan, "I'm not so sure another sleepless night would be good for me."

"I can take you to a place where we can smoke a pipe of opium. It will relax you and put you to sleep," Ivan purred.

"I'll drop my group at the hotel and meet you in the lobby in twenty minutes."

Charlotte took one look at Ivan's car and summoned an Uber. It looked like a can of tuna fish on wheels. She was taking no chances.

Their destination was the Respite, which was situated in a freestanding house in a questionable neighborhood. The façade of white brick was dirty, and a few unhealthy tendrils of ivy struggled to creep up the wall. Inside, to camouflage a miasma of smoke, red gels over the lights managed to create a festive ambiance, inviting and flattering. Enya-type music assaulted their ears.

Ivan seemed to be well known, however, and they lounged in a quasi-luxurious library setting, smoking one pipe. The snuffing out of all feeling and desire was as surprising and thrilling to Charlotte as the cocaine rush had been. She wanted another pipe but didn't want Ivan to know. "We should go." She barely managed to speak. "This is a reasonable hour for bed." Her lips felt thick and stiff.

Back in her room, Charlotte dropped into a deep and dreamless sleep, waking refreshed and happy to start the day. She promised herself she would get by on Percodan and cough syrup, waiting until later for whatever treat Ivan had in store for her.

But at the end of the day, Charlotte found Kay and Lilly waiting for her with garment bags in hand. "There's a reception for you in the Kremlin Armory. We brought changes of clothes for you and Gail," Kay said.

"I'd forgotten. Is my partner, Ivan, coming?"

"No, this is very small. Just our group and some officials. The rooms of the Almazny Fond in the armory are like a huge safe."

"But I want Ivan to join us." Charlotte was adamant.

"This a highlight of touring Moscow and a very special privilege to have it privately opened for us."

"What about dinner?"

"A private dinner is scheduled. We don't have information on that, only that the location is unspecified on the schedule."

Charlotte knew there was no point in arguing.

They entered the Kremlin through the wide arch under a tower designated as the Presidential Entrance and used only for special people at special times. The windowless rooms where the jewels were exhibited had Gothic ceilings, which gave an illusion of soaring height, but despite this, Charlotte felt claustrophobic. She had the distinct sensation she was going to swallow her tongue. As far as she knew, no one in her family had been elliptic, but the feeling was strong and sent her into a panic, her breath shallow and erratic.

Dmitri sensed she was in trouble and escorted her outside through the throng of officials and security personnel. During the short time they'd been in the armory, the Kremlin had melted into darkness, a half moon had risen in the clear night sky, and the air had turned brittle with cold.

Charlotte gasped, "I'm sorry. I don't know what happened to me in there."

"Drink this water, *Myshka,* and take a deep breath of good Russian air."

Charlotte, stooped over, moved closer to Dmitri and grasped the lapels of his overcoat. "I feel hunted and trapped."

"There, there, you don't have to go back. I'll go get the others, but let me get you to the car first."

Charlotte clutched his arm. "Don't leave me. Ask one of the chauffeurs to get them."

"Security will bring them out soon, anyway. We're due at the dacha at quarter to eight. Putin is very precise about time."

"This is a great honor for us to be invited. I want to be at my best. I wish I had something to pep me up."

"I'll send for some coffee."

Coffee? "Coffee won't do the trick. Maybe we could swing by the hotel, and I will pop up to my room and get something." Charlotte's voice was strained.

"The hotel is in the opposite direction. We don't have time for that."

"I can be quick."

"Putin is not a patient man, *Myshka.* And this is an unprecedented honor for a foreign ballerina."

"I know. I wish I had known this was on the agenda."

"They can't commit. Heads of State are busy people. One never knows until the last minute. They didn't want to disappoint us."

A large military helicopter flew them to the magnificent Italianate palace and the formal dinner proceeded without further incident. It was only by using her extreme self-discipline that Charlotte was able to hide feeling restless and irritable. She barely managed to present her public persona to the assembled luminaries *chez* Putin. She did not connect these feelings with drug use and began to worry she could be coming down with the flu.

Back in the lobby of the Metropol, Dmitri kissed Charlotte's hand. "Good night, my *Myshka*, you were superb tonight. Poised and elegant as always, and your Russian dazzled the President. What teacher has such a pupil?"

Charlotte laughed and curtsied to him as she dove into the elevator.

Only Kay and Lilly were aware of what the evening had cost her.

CHAPTER TWENTY-FIVE

Lilly and Charlotte were seated at the mahogany dining table in Charlotte's suite waiting for room service to come with breakfast. The paneling was painted a pale blue-green, and a large bunch of daffodils stood at attention in a clear glass vase in the center of the table, their sweet fragrance delicately scenting the air.

"Just take the nail polish off. It looks like you don't give a damn." Lilly always noticed but rarely commented on things like this.

"I don't have time. And in fact, I don't give a damn."

Room Service knocked. Kay called from her room to say she'd get the door and would join them later after her shower.

Lilly helped herself to kielbasa and pancakes. "You're on TV tonight, and you talk with your hands. Russian women will notice."

"Send someone to the theatre, then." Charlotte looked at her sister with glassy, bored eyes.

"Someone has been there everyday this week waiting for you. Ivan is always in your dressing room," Lilly remarked.

"You're just grumpy because you miss George."

"Don't bring George into this."

"We're in full dress rehearsal mode. I can have the manicure while I'm in the makeup chair. Sorry I embarrass you."

"Having dinner with Putin is a very big deal."

"No one knew we were having dinner with him."

"That's no excuse to be careless. Honestly, Charlotte, you know this is part of your job. What's the matter with you?"

"There are other things I'd rather do with my time. Like getting to know my partner. He had a bad breakup with Giselle and needs some kindness."

"Get the manicure."

"Message received, and though I hate to change this fascinating subject, I want to say how lucky we all are that Dmitri is here. We couldn't have gotten through last night without him."

"I know, and for the interview this evening, he'll be on the set with you."

"I heard. What a relief." Charlotte got up to leave.

"And Charlotte, a word to the wise, I don't think they call your partner Ivan the Terrible for no reason. I heard Giselle married her oligarch to get away from him. He has a bad reputation."

"Oh, please. Enough with the gossip. He's an incredible dancer who's been through a rough time."

"The suicide attempt was not about Giselle. I hear it was about owing big money to drug dealers, and Giselle's husband paid off his debts to get him off her back."

Charlotte blanched but spoke without pausing. "Lilly, it's not like you to give credence to this kind of talk. It's none of our business. Ivan is highly prized by the Bolshoi, and I enjoy his company." She turned her back on her sister and left the room, taking the moral high ground with her.

Kay crossed Charlotte in the hall. "I left three things on your bed. Before you leave, choose one for the interview, and I'll have it pressed."

"You choose, Mom. I've got to go."

"The interview will be at the theatre. I'll be there by five with the clothes."

"Okay, but maybe I'll wear one of the costumes."

"Bad idea. They want to interview Charlotte Darling, not Giselle."

"You win. See you later."

Charlotte left and Kay went into the dining room, picked up a croissant and sat opposite Lilly.

Kay said, "I overheard a bit and guess you've talked about Ivan's reputation."

"She's going to do as she pleases. You know that." Lilly pushed her plate away and picked up her embroidery hoop.

"You had to warn her. Thank God Dmitri's here. We would never have known."

"If Charlotte thinks about this, she'll know Dmitri's our source." Lilly held green silk threads up to the light and squinted.

"But she also knows he always has her best interest at heart." Kay put a glass of orange juice in front of Lilly.

"I don't know what she knows and doesn't know anymore. She's not been herself for months now. Ever since that night she had the meltdown and lost her hairpiece at the dinner table, she's been acting really weird. Even before that."

"Now, now. She's been under a lot of pressure. She wants to be the best Giselle. She wants the interview to go well and wants to speak Russian properly."

"Does she want that or do you?"

"I would say we all want that, don't we, Lilly? Don't we want Charlotte to excel at everything she sets her mind to?" Kay's tone was sharp.

"I think you see what you want to see."

"You do, too, dear."

Lilly dropped the sewing in her lap and contemplated the clouds painted on the ceiling for a moment. "Mark my words. This won't end well."

There was another knock at the door, and Priscilla appeared. Kay asked, "Have you been having fun, sweetie? Is Dmitri a good tour guide?"

"Perfect guide. Plus he makes me laugh. I couldn't be happier, but I don't think I've been much use to Mrs. D." She flopped down on the chair next to Lilly.

"Fasten your seatbelt. There'll be a lot of action after today's interview. And opening night is only two days away," Kay commented.

"You know the strange thing is, we've been here for over a week, and Mrs. D. hasn't asked for any of her usual foods. Do you think she's all right?"

"She's too busy," Kay answered, and Lilly looked up as if she wanted to say something.

Priscilla continued, "Marc Dubois, the photographer from Paris, wants to start shooting at seven tomorrow morning. He brought his makeup artist, stylist and PA with him. They'll be here at six. I have texted this to Mrs. D, but haven't heard from her. Can you make sure she knows?"

"You'll be there for the interview this afternoon, won't you?" Kay asked.

"Of course, but she's good at giving me the slip. I'm going to put a note in her room and leave one in her dressing room as well. But if you can speak to her, I'll feel better."

* * *

"It's written as plain as day on the schedule." Lilly piped in. "Charlotte never forgets things like that."

Ivan was in makeup at the same time as Charlotte. "I'll wait for you, and we can have dinner after the interview."

"I was hoping you'd say that. Some of the others might like to join us," Charlotte said.

"Get rid of them."

"I was hoping you'd say that, too."

"I want to get to know you better, Charlotte. I burn to know you better, to know you in a different way. You must feel that when we touch."

Charlotte looked pointedly at the makeup artists and manicurist.

"These girls don't speak English," Ivan sneered.

"But we've been speaking in Russian, until just now."

"You see what you do to me? Now the fire's gone to my brain. I don't even know what language I'm speaking."

The rehearsal was brilliant. The whole company was on a high, and even though it was hard for Charlotte to settle down for the interview, her habitual self-discipline came to her rescue. Everyone was pleased with the result.

"Let's go to Café Pushkin and celebrate." Dmitri was proud of his pupil.

"You all go ahead. I want to work on the first *pas de deux* with Ivan."

"Would you like me to stay?" Gail asked.

"Thanks, but Ivan and I can handle this alone."

"Mrs. D, don't forget Marc Dubois is expecting you at seven tomorrow morning for the perfume shoot, and his team arrives in your suite at six."

"I've got the schedule. Don't worry, Priscilla."

The group stood, shifting weight from one foot to the other. No one wanted to make the first move.

Charlotte made a shooing gesture. "Go on. Get out. Enjoy yourselves. Ivan and I have work to do."

Dmitri looked over his shoulder on the way out. "Take care of yourself, *Myshka*."

Room service knocked on the door at five-thirty the next morning. Kay answered wearing the hotel robe and then went to Charlotte's room while the waiter set the table.

Charlotte was dressed in yesterday's clothes lying face down on top of the bed, which had not been slept in. When Kay shook her by the shoulder, she moaned, "Give me ten more minutes."

Kay covered her with the duvet but said nothing.

There was another knock at the door. Kay opened the door to Lilly. "I think your sister has caught a chill. I want her to stay in bed until the last minute."

At ten of six Kay woke Charlotte. "You might want to take a shower, dear."

Charlotte stumbled into the bathroom and closed the door. Ten minutes later she was bright eyed and full of energy, talking a mile a minute, switching from fractured French to Russian with impressive ease.

By the time they all arrived in Red Square, Marc and his assistant had set up for the shoot with the glorious domes of St. Basil Cathedral in the background.

Charlotte was a true professional. She complied expertly with direction from Marc, and the shoot lasted only ninety minutes.

"Thank you, Madame Darling. I think Monsieur de Moret will be pleased with these shots for Tutu. I look forward to seeing you in Paris next month for the April in Paris shoot."

"Marc, you're a pleasure to work with. I trust you to Photoshop the hell out of these and come up with perfection."

As they were loading the equipment into the van, Marc remarked to his PA, "Let's hope she gets a good night's sleep before the next shoot. We were lucky today didn't call for close-ups."

"Yeah. She was pretty shaky this morning."

CHAPTER TWENTY-SIX

The ball at the Kremlin Palace went without a hitch, but two days later, three young paramedics stood looking down at Charlotte's nearly naked body. They were dressed in black, wearing combat boots more appropriate for military exercises than for emergency calls in luxury hotels. The mailroom of the Hotel Metropol was quiet. It was five a.m., and there she was, unconscious and lying in a laundry cart.

"Her vitals are okay, but we'd better wait for the cops before we move her. Posters of her are all over town. Last night she opened at the Bolshoi."

"That American dancer? What's she doing dumped back here?"

"Take her blood and get the night manager."

"I'm right here." The man walking into the room had on a dark suit and a blue tie.

Sirens screamed outside, and two uniformed policemen entered through the service door.

"What's going on here?" The police lieutenant took charge.

"Our security guard answered the alarm. The service door had been breached, and when he got here, our guest, Mrs. Darling, was lying on top of this cart full of sheets. The guard called the paramedics first, then you, then me. Two of her family members are here at the hotel."

"Tell them to meet us at the hospital," the police officer ordered and turned to the paramedics, "Put her in the ambulance and take her to the American Clinic pronto. My wife's got tickets to see her dance tonight."

"Lots of luck with that, Lieutenant," a paramedic said.

"Don't discount Dr. Kleper. He's familiar with raising the dead."

"Oh, yeah, that hot Brazilian guy," the female paramedic replied. "I was with him once when every member of a rock band was out of commission. And, you're right, he got them on stage in time."

Dr. Kleper met them in the emergency room. He was a tall healthy-looking man in his mid-thirties with black hair and pale gray eyes. A cursory drug screen showed opium only. He administered Naloxone intravenously, and Charlotte responded immediately. There were no marks on her body indicating a struggle and no evidence of a sexual assault.

By the time Kay and Lilly arrived, she was sitting up, dressed in a hospital gown. She couldn't meet her mother's eyes. "Mom, please get Priscilla to bring some clothes for me. I need shoes, too."

"Tell us what happened," Kay demanded.

Charlotte glanced at the doctor. He said, "Your daughter needs to speak to the police now."

Dr. Kleper bowed deeply from his slender waist. "I'll be back in half an hour to check on the patient. I'll bring a nasal spray of the antidote, which anyone can give her when there's a recurrence."

"What do you mean a recurrence? A recurrence of what, Doctor? My daughter . . ."

"Madame, I think you should be prepared." With that he spun on his heel and left the three women alone.

"Curt, but handsome," Lilly remarked.

"It's that Ivan," Kay started.

"Mom, please. Just call Priscilla so I can leave here as soon as possible."

Kay left the cubicle to make the call, and Lilly hovered over her sister.

"Lilly, I know what you're thinking. So do me a favor, and don't think out loud."

Lilly patted Charlotte's hand and sat down on the only chair. The awkward silence continued after Kay returned. Five minutes later, Kay inhaled sharply, preparing to speak.

Charlotte raised her hand. "Look, Mom, I was robbed. Not raped, just robbed. Let's drop it."

Two police detectives came in and asked Kay and Lily to leave the room. At the end of the interview with Charlotte, one of the detectives handed her a card and said, "If you can remember anything more, please give us a call."

"Just so you know, I won't be pressing charges. I don't want the press to get ahold of this."

"Thank you, Mrs. Darling. You can rely on our discretion."

The doctor arrived with Narcan spray and discharge papers only a few moments before Priscilla came with the clothes. The strained quiet continued in the taxi and in the elevator. And other than Kay's ordering breakfast, the suite was silent.

Finally, Priscilla said, "Call me when you need me." She went to her room and phoned Dmitri. "There's been some sort of incident with Mrs. Darling. I'm not sure what happened so don't ask me any questions, but you need to know it's possible she won't be able to dance tonight."

"What do you mean?"

"I think I can venture an opinion. Ivan can't be trusted." Priscilla sat on the edge of her bed.

"As I told you." Dmitri's voice coming through the receiver was firm.

"I'm not going to mention this to Gail. Anyway, I have no idea what happened, and I'm not sure the others do either. There's a ban on speech."

"Does she look strong enough to dance tonight?"

"She looks physically fine to me, but she seems surly. Something I've never seen in her before."

"Charlotte's a professional. She'll dance if she can. And you're right to warn me there could be a problem and also right in not bringing Gail into this."

"The storyline of the ballet gives me the creeps with Giselle dancing herself to death and then more dancing, post-mortem." Priscilla shivered.

"Now, Priscilla, don't go and get superstitious on me."

"Just saying. It's bizarre. No wonder City Ballet doesn't do it."

Charlotte danced brilliantly that night, but Kay and Lilly held their breaths wondering what she would do next.

Right after the performance, she gave Ivan a peck on the cheek and went straight to the stage door, where she autographed programs and posed for photographs with her fans for over an hour. Kay and Priscilla were by her side, and it was they who finally said, "Enough," and walked her across the square and up to her suite for a room service dinner.

Though Charlotte was bone tired, she had a long shower, and with the hot water pelting down, she thought over the events of the previous evening. As she told the police, she was certain she left the Respite alone and took a taxi to the hotel. She thought it was just a random taxi hailed by the doorman. She didn't remember anything after giving the driver the name of the hotel.

The police had it down as a robbery, and an extended toxicology report would tell if there was something other than opium in her system. To be honest with herself, she knew she probably passed out in the taxi and the driver had helped himself. She also knew she was lucky not to have been raped.

There was not a whisper of misstep in the press, and Charlotte made herself unapproachable on the subject to her family and friends. So the details of the previous evening remained mysterious.

The next morning, Dr. Kleper called her and said her unconsciousness was caused by an overdose of opium. He recommended she carry Narcan in her purse.

Charlotte kept herself in check for a few more nights, sticking strictly to the schedule and was, as always, precisely on time for every event. But the sweet smell of opium called to her like a siren song. Several times during the following week, she managed to slither over to the Respite with Ivan, leaving after one pipe and congratulating herself on self-restraint.

After rehearsal at the end of the week, Ivan walked Charlotte from the theatre to the hotel. "I've got something special planned for us after the last performance. I know it'll be a first for you." His half smile was provocative.

"It'll have to be the night before the last performance. I have a business associate coming, and we leave for Paris right after the final curtain call."

"It's not ideal to perform the day after this particular treat, but we're indestructible, aren't we?"

Charlotte had not told Ivan about her trip to the hospital.

Indestructible? Well, maybe not, she thought, but replied, "Of course. And what does this particular treat involve?"

"The private rooms at the Respite."

"Did you say rooms, with an 's'?"

"Yes."

"Don't tell me it's a cast party."

"Certainly not. No more questions."

"Ivan, I'll miss you too much, and I'd invite you to New York, but I have no idea where to find the delights you're used to."

"I can find anything anywhere. I'll introduce you to your own city."

"How about right after *Nutcracker*?"

"I'll be there in time to see you dance it. Or better yet, why don't you arrange for me to dance Drosselmeyer for a week? We could be the twenty-first century Nureyev and Fontaine."

"Oh, what a clever boy you are! And then you can stay on for a couple of weeks. We'll go to Palm Beach for a while."

"Tempting." He caressed her shoulder as she entered the Metropol but left without seeing the look of distaste on her face.

CHAPTER TWENTY-SEVEN

The private rooms at the Respite were off the central hall and consisted of a large sitting room, dining room and two bedrooms, both with double king-sized beds. A soundproof-mirrored door separated these rooms from the rest of the club. When this door opened, a different world appeared. Inside, a perfect balance of sinister and sensational awaited them. Purple light shone on sheets of opium smoke, floating like ghosts through the stale air. Charlotte hesitated at the entrance.

"I offer you the cream of the crop!" Ivan said as laughter spilled out into the hall. She stepped over the threshold.

Twenty of the most glamorous and debauched of the city's beauty elite were there to greet Charlotte. The dining room table was spread with caviar, *foie gras* and smoked salmon as well as a five-star selection of illegal substances, all surrounding a nude girl posing Roman-style, eating grapes. The hour was late, and all of the assembled were already under the influence of various chemicals, and the room pulsated with percussion.

The atmosphere was upbeat, and the gilded and polished glitterati of Moscow draped themselves over each other in various states of dress and undress, chatting and moving to the rhythm of the room.

"I want to encase your beautiful body with desire, and I have some excellent E here to help do the job for me. How would you like it?" Ivan put his arm around Charlotte's shoulder.

"I'm fine for the moment. And I don't think I want to try anything new tonight. How about a couple of lines and then a pipe before bed?" Charlotte ferreted in her purse for the pack of Marlboros and lit one with a shaking hand, lingering on the periphery of the group like an impostor.

"But I have all these gorgeous creatures here for you to choose from. This is what a first class love-fest looks like."

"But, Ivan, we have a matinee and an evening performance tomorrow. Plus, I leave for Paris. I can't pull an all-nighter."

"Let's do some coke and see what happens."

Charlotte was anxious to get to the drug and had a bit more than before. Immediately she felt invincible and the feeling of trepidation slipped away like an anchor over the side of a boat. Her attention was caught by a pair of fine-boned twin boys dancing to a different beat. Watching her watch them, Ivan commented, "We can't hear their music."

The first hour flew by, and Ivan was back at her side. "Come with me to a bedroom and watch. You may want to change your mind about the E when you see."

Charlotte tensed. "I'm fine, really. Just another line. And some Perrier."

Ivan didn't push it, and Charlotte unwound, sipping her water only to find half an hour later consciousness was slipping away. Forcing her eyes to focus, she searched for Ivan in the two front rooms. Not finding him, she summoned all her strength and lurched to the reception desk.

"I hate to leave this party, but I need to get to the American Clinic. Please call and ask for Dr. Kleper. My name is Charlotte Darling."

The girl behind the desk looked inquiringly at the security guard. He nodded and said, "Everything's under control here. I'll drive her over. Go ahead and call the clinic."

Charlotte was losing muscle control and had to be helped into the car by two pairs of hands. She was overcome by emotion, telling them over and over how much she appreciated their help.

By the time they reached the clinic, Dr. Kleper took one look at her and said, "Get a drug screen and keep her hydrated."

The patient was sweating and agitated, jabbering constantly through clenched teeth and twitching erratically.

The screen picked up MDMA and cocaine. An intravenous flush was started right away.

"Please don't notify my family, dear, dear Dr. Kleper," was the first coherent thing Charlotte said.

"Mrs. Darling, all of Moscow knows your final performances are today." His left wrist shot out from his lab coat, and he looked down at his watch. "The curtain goes up in twelve hours, isn't that right?"

"Yes."

"How can you be so careless of your health, your career, the people who love you and those who look up to you? You're the idol of so many young girls all over the world. It's shameful to disrespect your talent and position like this."

Charlotte gasped. No American doctor would have dared talk to a patient like this, she thought. Both doctor and patient were flushed with anger.

Kleper looked down at her, lying helpless on the gurney. "I'll do my best to get you on stage by two o'clock, but it's your responsibility to stay clean. The path you're on leads straight to the morgue."

Never had anyone spoken to Charlotte Darling like this.

By seven a.m. Charlotte felt well enough to call Kay. "Mom, I felt my heart racing this morning so I came to the hospital to have Dr. Kleper check me out. Everything's fine. Just nerves."

"I'll be there in fifteen minutes."

"Don't worry. He's going to do an echocardiogram, to make sure, and I'll go to the Bolshoi from here. Concentrate on the packing."

"Charles is arriving in time for lunch."

"Tell him I'm busy at the theatre. Will he be at both performances?"

"Of course."

"Have him come backstage after the matinee. And don't mention anything to anyone."

"Rest, then dance, Charlotte, and I'll take care of everything else."

Charles de Moret arrived looking fresh even after his three and a half hour flight from Paris. He enjoyed his lunch with Kay in the hotel dining room and didn't think it odd that Charlotte was unavailable.

They walked to the theatre and sat in house seats. During intermission, Charles looked very serious. "Kay, I was truly alarmed at how convincing the death dance was. And she's so thin. Is she alright?"

"She's fine."

"I don't think much of the male lead. He looked clumsy to me."

"He's much worse than clumsy. She's expecting you backstage after the next act. You'll probably bump into him. Ignore him. He's big trouble."

"What's been going on?"

"I think he's giving her drugs."

"What kind of drugs?"

"I don't know, but she's not herself. Coming in and going out at all hours. She doesn't want you to know. So don't mention it."

"I'm glad you warned me."

"Just make sure she's not around any bad influences in Paris."

"My friends aren't into that."

At the end of the second act, the applause was halfhearted. A French couple seated behind Charles and Kay remarked how disappointed they were that the principal dancers were sloppy and seemed fatigued. Not what they expected of the renowned Bolshoi.

In response to Charles's knock on her dressing room door, Charlotte called out, "Get in here!"

He opened the door to find her bent over the mirrored table inhaling a line of cocaine. She stood abruptly and turned to face him with a look of surprise on her face, which turned quickly to defiance.

"I know what you are going to say, Charles. Save it. I don't care what you think. I *need* this to dance. No one my age can do this twice a day without help."

"How long has this been going on?"

"I don't want to discuss it. Leave me alone. I'll sleep on the plane and be ready for the perfume business tomorrow. It won't interfere with your plans for me."

As he was leaving, Ivan came in. "Is this the guy from Paris?"

"He's on his way out."

Charles went to the bar at the Metropol and called Kay's room. "Charlotte dismissed me like a school boy. I see what you mean. She's not herself."

"Swear yourself to secrecy. She's been to the hospital twice since we arrived here."

"Did she have a good doctor?"

"Excellent. Dr. Kleper. At the American Clinic."

"I'm going to talk to him."

"Don't ever let Charlotte know. She gets so cross if I do anything she considers meddling. I think he'll recommend drug rehab, but understand this, Charles, that is O-U-T. Her face is too well-known, and it would ruin everything she's worked for her entire life."

"I hear you. We wouldn't want a junkie as the face for our perfumes, either. That's for sure."

"Don't even say things like that. She's an incredible athlete and artist. She can't be a junkie. There was never any problem before we came to Moscow, and Ivan the Terrible became her best friend."

"Look, Kay, I'm going to try to see this doctor. I may not make the performance tonight, so I'll meet you at the airport. I'll leave the tail numbers for our plane with the concierge. We're scheduled for takeoff at midnight. Send the suitcases anytime, and be sure to let the pilots know the names of everyone coming with us to Paris and what passport they hold for the manifest."

"Okay, Charles, good luck. I hope you manage to see Dr. Kleper. He's a busy man."

Charles didn't bother to call for an appointment and after leaving instructions for Kay, he took the first taxi to the American Clinic, only to find that the doctor had left at noon and was not expected back for a month. Charles's good looks and Gallic charm helped him get the doctor's cell number. The two men arranged to meet downstairs at Café Pushkin.

Dr. Kleper knew a lot about addiction, which he defined as continued use of a substance despite mounting negative consequences. He told Charles that Kay was mistaken if she thought this was a new problem. He was sure she'd been abusing mood-altering substances for quite some time.

A long discussion and many phone calls later, a plan was hatched. Kleper would come with them to Paris. Charles didn't want Charlotte to go to the hotel in her current condition and made arrangements for them to go directly his brother's house in Normandy to stay for a month.

Charles cancelled all photography and interviews in Paris and arranged for his osteopath to visit Charlotte at the house once a week for the coming month. An excellent Thai masseur lived in a nearby village whose partner did acupuncture. Their services were reserved three times a week. In two hours the men had created a private rehab for Charlotte.

Kleper's vacation would be a working one.

CHAPTER TWENTY-EIGHT

As Charlotte boarded the Gulfstream V, she greeted Charles coolly, then noticed Dr. Kleper comfortably seated, reading *After On,* an exciting novel by Rob Reid, about artificial intelligence.

"Going to Paris on vacation, Doctor?" she asked consciously trying to make her voice sound innocent and cheerful.

"Not exactly. I'm off to Normandy for a month in the country. Are you pleased with your triumph in Moscow?"

"I'm already on to Paris." Charlotte was still cranked from applause and coke. She wanted to enjoy this, but the sight of the doctor was ominous. She had some Ambien in her purse. Did she dare take it? All she wanted now was to sleep and sleep and have all this over when she awoke, refreshed and renewed and clean and in her bed on 71st Street.

This desire was intense, although the chances of realizing it were zero. She stood, immobilized, at the entrance to the cabin. Desperation adjusted itself around her like a thick woolen cloak, ruining her high.

Suddenly, the tears came. Charles went to her and held her close. She relaxed into him and sobbed. Surprised to feel comfort in his arms, she let go completely.

Kay, Lilly and Priscilla boarded and silently found their places. The uniformed steward entered from the cockpit. "Monsieur de Moret, we've been cleared for takeoff."

Charles maneuvered Charlotte onto the taupe leather sofa, sat beside her and fastened her seatbelt. The sleek jet darted forward.

When they landed in Paris, Kay and the doctor went with a docile Charlotte to Normandy. She'd sobbed for hours on the plane. She was empty now. The fight had gone.

Charles promised he'd come for the weekend. Lilly and Priscilla would continue traveling on to New York until needed in Paris for the Tutu launch. As they were saying their goodbyes, Priscilla handed over a small case of Charlotte's junk food to Kay saying, "If she needs anything else, email me." Priscilla was clutching a rumpled bag from Elena Yarmak containing a black lambskin ushanka, which she felt certain her father would never wear unless badgered into it by her determined mother.

The sky was gray in Normandy and a light rain was falling when Charlotte woke up at noon the next day. She recalled committing to an open mind last night. Okay, she thought, she'd listen to Dr. Kleper with one ear. The good news was, so far, he hadn't demanded her supply. Breathing a sigh of relief, she reached for her purse and found to her shock the pills were gone.

Diving out of bed and ripping through her suitcases, she rifled each purse, bag and container. Nothing in any of them. She dressed and rushed down the limestone stairs, pausing at the bottom step and listening intently. There were muffled voices off to her left. After walking through two large sitting rooms, she finally found the library. Kay and the doctor were seated on sofas facing each other. Whatever they were discussing came to an abrupt halt when Charlotte entered the room.

"I'm glad you were able to sleep," Kleper said.

"When did you search my things?"

"I examined them in the hall before they were sent up to your room. You were already asleep, or I would've told you what I was doing. Believe me this is for your own good."

"I have excellent doctors in New York who are aware of my medical history who prescribe specific medications 'for my own good'. You don't know me at all. How *dare* you take my meds?"

"I called all the prescribing physicians while you were sleeping, and I'm certain detoxing from these chemicals will benefit you."

"I hate you both!" Charlotte stamped her foot. Desperation, anger and fear flooded her brain. She approached her mother, fists raised, with the obvious intention of striking. The doctor intervened, roughly pushing her arms down to her side and firmly moving her towards the door.

He told her, "The acupuncturist is coming at two. Right now there's detox tea for you in the kitchen, and I want you to eat the meal, which has been prepared."

"Why should I go along with this outrage?"

"Last night you agreed to keep an open mind. As of now, you've been awake for less than an hour, and you've already shown signs of violent behavior. Don't you think it's time to take a look at yourself?"

Charlotte managed an apathetic, "Fuck you, Dr. Kleper," and trailed behind him towards the distant kitchen.

"The meals and teas I've ordered will help the detox process as will acupuncture and massage. After the acupuncture, you'll need a nap and then the massage is at five."

"Thank God I won't have to talk to you."

"Not today. And I can arrange to have your dinner sent to your room, if you'd like. Tomorrow you and I will start the day with a long walk together."

"I'd call the cops, if I could speak the language well enough. And just so we're clear here, I'm *not* a consenting adult in this charade." Charlotte noticed her command of French had diminished significantly without the assistance of cocaine.

"You're free to leave."

"I noticed that I have no money and no ID as well as no medication. This must be illegal."

"It's time for you to grow up. And I'm going to help you."

Charlotte took a swing at the doctor, but he blocked her arm. "You need to detox," he said.

She loathed him but acknowledged on some level he was right.

The next morning Charlotte dragged herself out of bed and stood at her open bedroom window admiring the formal garden of shaped boxwood and tailored lawns. A pale gray mist swept the landscape. Jumping back into bed, she thought of the last forty-eight hours and shivered, shocked at the depth drugs had taken her to in such a short time.

By the time she was dressed, Dr. Kleper was waiting for her at the bottom of the staircase with cup of medicinal tea.

"If you're hungry, have a croissant. Otherwise, drink this and let's get going."

She swallowed the bitter brew and grimly set out trailing the doctor and gritting her teeth.

An hour later, the sun made a brief appearance as they walked up the gravel drive to the stately house. Fragile sunbeams mingled with dense mist. A perfect metaphor, Charlotte thought, smirking at the irony.

She had to admit, the walk had had some merit. She found Dr. Kleper's straightforward style astounding, accustomed as she was to minced words, bland and sanitized.

Charles's osteopath, Anne-Sophie, arrived in her vintage MG right after lunch. She interviewed Charlotte and gave her a treatment. It was amazing how quickly the aches and pains were relieved. The patient slept around the clock that night. Though she still felt depressed, she sensed her physical health returning.

Charles arrived on Saturday morning and was pleased to see that even though Charlotte was still too thin and apathetic, her skin had a healthy glow. On Sunday morning, he said, "Come with me to Mass. There's a wonderful medieval church walking distance from here."

"I'm not Catholic, and I don't speak French."

"God doesn't care that you're a heathen, and the walk will do you good."

"What about the 'don't speak French' part?"

"The vibration is healing. Think of it as sound therapy."

She went with him, and he was right. Whatever it was did her good.

By the beginning of the second week Charlotte's anger and depression had dissipated, and she began to notice first the garden, then the architecture of the lovely old house. She was responding well to all her therapies and appreciated the emerging clarity of mind.

At the end of that week Charles arrived brandishing a fistful of tickets.

"The circus is in town! It's the family one that comes to this part of the world every spring. I've gone to it every year since I was small. We'll go tonight *and* tomorrow afternoon!"

All color drained out of Charlotte's face, and Kay looked nervous. Dr. Kleper was attuned to his patient's every reaction, and his antenna was up. Charles blathered on unaware and declared he would be including the whole staff in his invitation.

Kleper took Charles aside and said he didn't think Charlotte should go. He would stay home with her. That night Kay went with the others, and Charlotte was able to talk freely with the doctor.

"I have always hated the circus. I think it's because Mom's freaked out by acrobats, and I inherited her phobia."

"I think it's more than that."

"Well, I have a horror of clowns."

"Why do you think that is?"

"I don't know. I just think they're creepy. More than creepy, really. I'm frightened of them. Mimes, too."

Kleper wondered if that could somehow be the source of her frigidity. She'd recently told him about that. It was something he knew little about but wanted to help. "Would you mind having hypnosis? It might be very interesting for you to know why you're frightened of clowns."

"If you think it's a good idea, then I'm in."

On Sunday morning, Charlotte was looking forward to going to Mass again with Charles and found, to her surprise, she felt familiar with the simple stone church and the rhythm of the liturgy. She liked the monochrome bareness of the interior contrasted to the rich color and pattern of the stained glass windows. It was cool, quiet and immaculately clean. "I see why you like to come here."

"I've known this place all my life, and I'll be buried here."

"So morbid."

"Not really. We all exit the planet one day, and I like choosing my blast-off point."

That afternoon, Kay managed to get out of circus-round-two, and stayed home with Charlotte.

"I can't believe you went, Mom."

"I know how to close my eyes."

"Believe me, I know how you feel. Not to change the subject, but I need your advice on something. Dr. Kleper wants me to have hypnosis. What do you think?"

"I don't have any personal experience, but Nina had a few sessions years ago. She said it was effective for her. Do you want to call her?"

"No. She'll be thinking about the future now, not the past. I'm going to say yes. What's the harm?"

"Kleper is a good doctor. You can trust him."

During the doctor-patient walk on Monday morning, Charlotte said, "Mom doesn't know I have sexual issues, and it's better if it stays that way."

"Don't worry. I would never betray confidentiality. Your mother is a lovely woman, but she's been a classic enabler for you. I think you see that now, don't you?"

"Yes, but she has always had the right intentions."

"Indeed she does. You're blessed to have such a loyal ally in life."

"She said our friend Nina had success with hypnotherapy, and I'm looking forward to starting."

"I hope you won't mind if I sit in on the sessions."

"Of course not. I want to get to the bottom of this even more than you do."

CHAPTER TWENTY-NINE

There was no shortage of hypnotists practicing in Paris, but luckily Anne-Sophie knew one in Chartres, a nearby cathedral town. This man was intrigued by the case and agreed to see Charlotte on Wednesday morning.

Two sessions were required, but the upshot was that when Charlotte was five she was at the circus with her pregnant mother. Kay was experiencing an anxiety attack during the high wire act, and little Charlotte ran off to say hello to a beckoning clown.

He crouched down to her level, clasped her to him and slipped his hand inside her panties. He did this only six feet from Kay, in front of the entire audience. It was brief but brutal.

Kay never knew. She thought Charlotte was overtired and crying for more cotton candy. Kay went into labor later that afternoon, and Charlotte never told a soul. She didn't know how, and no one ever noticed the specks of blood.

After Charlotte came out of the trance, both doctors and patient spent an hour talking about this. Once she remembered it consciously as well as unconsciously, she agreed that the adult Charlotte could leave this incident in the past and not allow it to color her relationships with men for the rest of her life.

Charlotte and Kleper left the therapist's office and walked through the town towards the cathedral. "With the excitement of Lilly's birth and the trauma of my father's death, no wonder I repressed it. But trust me, I'm never going to go to a circus or watch a mime ever again," she said.

"There is no reason you'd have to." Kleper was pleased with his patient's mature attitude and her ability to see this as something she could let go of now that she saw what it was.

"Having this knowledge is like wearing a magic charm around my neck. Being able to remember and accept what happened is liberating. Thank you so much, Doctor K."

"I hope you can now be able to feel the joy of being chemical-free, as well."

They had coffee at the café facing the cathedral and continued discussing the session before driving back to the house.

What she didn't expect was a crying jag during her acupuncture session later that afternoon. The acupuncturist didn't question her. It was as if such outbursts were the norm.

Later Charlotte reported this to Kleper and added, "I feel cleansed as if those tears washed away the stains. And the poison."

"They say tears are purifying."

"Speaking of being pure, I want you to know I'm glad to be off pills. My thinking was skewed, and then when I added cocaine and opium to the mix, I was like Alice falling down the rabbit hole. Thank you for breaking my fall."

"All your thanks should go to Monsieur de Moret. It was his idea. He arranged for everything."

"I'll thank him. I'll thank him from the bottom of my heart."

Charlotte thought about Charles for the rest of the day. She remembered all the fun they'd had together over the past twenty years when they'd been first colleagues, then friends. She reminded herself that without Charles, she'd still be in physical pain and mental confusion. He was the one who organized osteopathy and acupuncture treatments. He was the one who'd convinced Dr. Kleper to spend his time, talent and vacation cleaning her up. No man loved her more than Charles. She was sure of it. His actions had proved it.

By bedtime she began to fantasize about him sexually and found she was not revolted. And on hearing that Charles had family obligations keeping him in Paris that weekend, her disappointment was out of proportion to what a friend without benefits would feel.

Over the ensuing days her bedtime thoughts of Charles went from not revolted to highly interested. This must be lust, she thought. She smiled more now and her interest in beauty returned. Not only was she aware of her body, but she began taking an interest in her clothes and hair, even going into the village for a manicure. Her dance routines were joyous now. Happiness was dawning.

Charles arrived the following Friday night bursting with news. "I have a lot to tell you!"

"You look very happy about something." Charlotte was beaming.

"I *am.* Very happy, indeed! Paulette and I are getting back together."

Charlotte blanched. "Your ex-wife?"

"Yes! At our daughter's twenty-fifth birthday party last week, she told me she'd made a mistake in leaving me and wants to get married again."

"But you can't do that!"

"Why ever not?"

"Because that never works. Look at Richard Burton and Elizabeth Taylor. And . . . and countless others."

"It'll be fine. And if it's alright with you, we'll have the reception here in the middle of August. You'll be renting the place then, but don't worry, Paulette will make all the arrangements. There'll be nothing for you to do but look beautiful—something you do so well."

"I can't believe you're making such a big change so quickly."

"Not such a big change. We were married for twenty-five years, only divorced for three. She's a very attractive woman and a meticulous housekeeper, who is well acquainted with all my idiosyncrasies. I could do a lot worse."

"But marriage? Why don't you live together and see how it works?"

"Paulette doesn't want to do that. She has her mind made up on marriage. She hates being single."

"What about the perfume launch?"

"We have everything we need for Tutu and can put April in Paris on hold. We'll do the photo shoot in the studio. It doesn't have to be April, you know."

"I was hoping I could do it while I'm here."

"You'll be back in July and August. We have plenty of time."

"My month is almost up. Will you come for the final weekend?"

"No, *cherie.* And I'm leaving you after dinner tonight. I have to look after my bride-to-be. But July will be here before you know it, and we'll see each other then. All this is new, and Paulette wants us to spend some time alone."

I bet she does, thought Charlotte. "I'm disappointed not to see her."

"She said to give you her best and that she knew you would understand. We leave for Italy in the morning. Ten days at the Villa d'Este. A pre-honeymoon."

"And what about Mass on Sunday?"

"I'll go in Italy."

"What a lucky woman Paulette is. I wish you both every good thing life has to offer. You've literally saved my life, and I'll be eternally grateful to you, my precious friend."

Charlotte managed to keep a brave face though dinner, but as soon as Charles left, she flew up to her room and grabbed a large bag of M&M Almonds. After scarfing down a couple of slugs, she found Dr. Kleper. He refused her offer of candy but accepted the invitation for a moonlight stroll.

She crunched on the chocolate covered nuts while telling him the story of her fantasies and describing the crushing blow of Charles's going back to his former wife.

"It's very healthy for a woman of your age to have sexual interests, and as for choosing Charles, that's only natural, too."

"But I feel like a jilted lover. I feel like he's been unfaithful to me."

"You know this love affair was only in your mind, not Charles's?"

"I do, but it doesn't seem to staunch the bleeding."

"You are a beautiful, talented woman. Many men will want to take Charles's place. You have to give yourself some time to heal from addiction and sexual repression."

"I feel like I have lead in my veins, but strangely, I don't feel like going back to pills. I owe that to you."

"This worked because you were willing. You did what was suggested and didn't cheat. I'm proud of you."

"So much is new for me now. I've never felt this way about a man before. I've never had sexual fantasies or felt a physical desire until last week."

"Give yourself time. These are early days."

"What will I do when our time is up? Can I do this without you?"

"Of course you can."

"Would it be possible for you to extend your stay here another two weeks?" Charlotte's voice was weak.

"I could arrange that, but don't you have a friend getting married soon?"

"Nina's wedding is tomorrow. I feel so bad missing it. But I need to be here. She's getting married in my garden in Palm Beach. My daughter and Lilly are there. They'll send lots of photos to Mom and me."

"Too bad there's no Wifi in the house so that you could feel more connected to the wedding."

"It's okay. I need to concentrate on what we're doing, and anyway, I love going down to the café with my computer everyday. I like the routine we've gotten into."

During the rest of her stay in Normandy, Charlotte began to notice late spring unfurl into early summer. Everyday brought new birds, and buds became flowers. The sky became a brighter blue, and the sun tinted her face. In the mornings, after walking with Kleper, she gathered blossoms and arranged them in porcelain vases she'd found in a kitchen cabinet. Despite her sadness about the non-romance, a sense of wellbeing was developing.

Acupuncture, osteopathy, massages and nutritious food had made a discernible difference in her body; the level of pain and the number of aches were diminished. Dr. Kleper and the hypnotist had transformed her thinking, and those two Sundays attending Mass with Charles had made her aware that a spiritual practice was missing in her life. As a way to start, she enlisted Kay and the doctor to walk with her to the small stone church on Sunday mornings. Sitting on the hard wooden pew and hearing the ancient words was a healing balm to her. Sound therapy, Charles had called it.

CHAPTER THIRTY

Priscilla was at the airport to meet Charlotte and Kay. In the car heading for Manhattan, she talked nonstop about mundane issues, which had occurred while Charlotte was in France. Tandem Hall wanted the last chapter, Dmitri wanted to continue Russian breakfasts at no charge, the June issue of *House Sensational* was out with pictures of Jasmine showing off Seventh Heaven, and Jasmine had posted pictures of the Newport garden on the Internet.

"She put red and yellow annuals in your perennial border. It's terrible," Priscilla announced.

"I'm sure it is. Please don't make me look."

"Also, Doctor King called saying you'd missed an appointment. He wants to know when you'll be back. I told him I didn't know."

"I'll get back to him. Anything else? As in, is there something interesting going on with Dr. Ellis and Lilly?"

"My psychic abilities, meager though they are, report an emphatic, 'Yes'. He went to Palm Beach for the wedding."

"Did you go, Priscilla? I didn't see any pictures of you."

"At the last minute, I came down with a stomach thing. Can't take stomach things anywhere."

"Definitely not," Charlotte grimaced.

"The honeymooners called from Rome. They're at the Hassler with a terrace overlooking the Spanish Steps. They said to tell you they've thought of you at the top of all seven hills."

"I can't wait to talk to the bride," Kay exclaimed. "The wedding pictures were fabulous. Who did the flowers?"

"Someone Topsy found."

"Topsy organizing flowers! Will wonders never cease?"

"Oh, and, Mrs. D., everyone in PR is thrilled with the reaction to the *Vain Fare* article announcing their cookbook. They featured your recipes, and apparently, several restaurants are serving your favorite, calling it 'Darling Charlotte's Cake'."

They chatted on, never once mentioning the reason for Charlotte's stay in France.

It was nearly five by the time they got to the apartment. Lilly and Topsy were there, and the place was filled with flowers. Gani had thought of everything including the famous cake.

In the morning, Charlotte called Dr. King and went to see him that same afternoon. After recounting what had happened in Moscow and Normandy, she said, "Those first two weeks off pills were hell. Complete and utter hell. I want to be sure to see you twice a week before leaving for France next month. I'm determined to stay away from all mood altering substances, and I think checking in with you is a good idea."

"I agree. Addiction is a subtle foe."

Charlotte settled down to finish her memoir. Casting her mind back to the yearlong divorce, she couldn't believe how detached she'd been. Getting Lilly on the phone, she said, "You know the divorce period is sort of a blur to me. It's like it was Mom's divorce, not mine. I didn't feel anything. I haven't felt anything for years. Maybe I need to apologize to Colin for being absent from our marriage."

"You weren't that bad. You two always seemed very happy with each other."

"It was an act. What about Topsy? How was I as a mother?"

"You had a demanding career, but honestly, you were pretty good until lately. You haven't been yourself for the last couple of years."

"I'm not going to ask you to explain what you mean by that, but I want you to know that I'm clean now and want to be the best sister-mother-daughter I can be to you, Topsy and Mom."

"Learn from the past and get on with it. Know I love you and am glad you are off the meds."

"Do you want to go to church with me on Sunday?"

"What?"

"I went with Charles a couple of times in Normandy and then a few times with Mom. Maybe it's better in French, but I liked it."

"Thanks anyway, but I'm spending the weekend with George. Call Dmitri. He goes to the Orthodox Church on 93rd Street and the service is in Russian. You might like that."

"Okay," she said and got back to the task at hand. She wrote truthfully about her disconnectedness during the divorce and described how she deceived and manipulated her family and staff. Then she continued with another chapter recounting her experiences in Moscow and the healing in France.

Charlotte worked for two weeks on those final chapters. She stopped only for appointments with Dr. King. She hadn't even called Dmitri. Once she'd finished, she invited Lilly for a reading.

Charlotte brought her laptop to the library, and while Lilly worked on her embroidery, Charlotte read. She paused and finished her Perrier before reading the final paragraphs.

> "In Normandy, I came face-to-face with myself. I assessed the collateral damage and came to believe I could go forward without causing any more harm. Perhaps, I can be a force for good. At this writing, I still don't know what that could be, but I now have the sacred gift of clarity. Surely there's a way for me to enrich the lives of others.

> Dr. Kleper said all religions and philosophies have at their core one simple concept. Examine yourself and help others. I have taken step one. It was painful at times. Counting the hours of my life spent under the influence of chemicals was a shocker. All those hours added up to years of being stuck in my own head. Unavailable to myself, unavailable to others, unavailable to life.
>
> The good doctor told me although I can't change the past, I can change the future and being clean makes the world a little bit better. I don't know if the world is any better, but something happened while I was in Normandy, and now I know I can be useful. I can be part of the solution instead of being the problem. Serenity has seeped in and stilled the chaos in my mind."

There was a brief silence after Charlotte closed her laptop. When Lilly spoke, her voice was thick with emotion, "I'm deeply touched by this, but my advice is to keep it private. Read it to Topsy and Mom. It'll mean the world to them. Keep the chapter that Tandem wants about the divorce. The truth is you *were* incapable of dealing with the divorce at the time and Mom took over. You don't need to go into the 'whys'. And I loved what you wrote about Colin and Jasmine in the tabloids and following them on Facebook and Twitter. That's what happened. But let the book end there."

"You've always had a level head, Lilly. I'll think about it over the weekend."

"Don't let it all hang out, like on daytime TV. You'd probably lose your licensing contracts."

"We each have such poignant stories. It's no wonder reality TV is so riveting."

"The riveting part of your story should stay in the family. There are enough celebrities who come forward about addiction. Maybe the world doesn't need to hear about yours. Maybe your fans need to think of you as pristine. Maybe that is your gift to them—living up to your own reputation."

"An undeserved reputation dreamed up by PR."

"But an inspiration to many. Let it be deserved now."

They said goodnight. Lilly went to George's, and Charlotte sat alone in the library and smoked while she reread the final chapter and thought about what Lilly had said.

I guess this is my last Marlboro, she thought, as she dropped the half-smoked cigarette into an ashtray. It's hard to walk the walk. But Charlotte knew the mathematical distance between hard and impossible is infinite, even though it doesn't feel that way sometimes.

Charlotte looked at her watch. Nine-thirty. Not too late to call.

"*Privet,* Dmitri. May I join you for church tomorrow?"

"Ah, *Myshka.* It would be a pleasure for me."

"For me, too."

"I can pick you up in twelve hours."

"I'll be ready."

The idea of an affair with Dmitri whizzed through her mind. No, she thought, not a good idea. At least not while Charles is still unmarried.

CHAPTER THIRTY-ONE

Monday afternoon found Charlotte comfortably horizontal on Dr. King's sofa. She was on her back, knees bent with a cushion under her head.

"I guess you could say I think about sex all the time now. I even considered jumping into the sack with my Russian language teacher, and I think about Charles every night. I've begun to wonder about Lilly's sex life, too. I don't know if this is normal or not. I just never thought about any of this before."

"Does it interfere with your daily life in any way?"

"No, but it's on my mind. Especially when thinking about Charles."

"What feelings does his impending marriage bring up for you?"

"I'm sad. I think it was a tragic cosmic timing error."

"Are you anxious about seeing him again?"

"Sort of. I feel rejected."

"But he had no idea you had romantic feelings for him, did he?"

"No, but still."

"Anything else you'd like to discuss?"

"I'm going to set up a grant-giving foundation. I want to do something to help dancers who've dedicated their lives to their art and need to change careers once the physical stress has taken its toll."

"Has this been a lifelong ambition?"

"It's a new idea. Dr. Kleper planted the seed."

They discussed this topic and then came back to the Charles situation. At the end of the session, Charlotte said, "I'll get through the summer. I've rented the house in Normandy, which belongs to Charles's brother. You know, where I was with Dr. Kleper. I won't be bored. And I have *The Nutcracker* and my foundation to look forward to in the fall."

"Call me anytime, if you feel like talking."

"They say money can't buy happiness, but it *can* rent houses. How can I stay unhappy with all my friends and family coming to visit?"

And so they parted for the summer. Charlotte walked from Beekman Place to 71st Street, yearning for Charles with every step.

She went directly to Priscilla's office. As she reached the door, the phone rang. Charlotte heard, "Mrs. Darling's line. Yes, sir. She just walked in. Hold on, please."

Priscilla covered the receiver with her hand and mouthed, "It's Mr. de Moret."

Charlotte inhaled deeply and held her breath. Still standing, she reached for the phone, exhaled as calmly as possible and said, "Charles, how lovely to hear from you."

"I'm calling to admit you were right. Richard Burton, Elizabeth Taylor and I were wrong."

"Things didn't work out?"

"Comic understatement, my dear."

Charlotte laughed for the first time in weeks. "What happened?"

"Let's say there were reasons for our divorce, and nothing's changed."

"I'll be there next week to distract you."

"I'll meet you at the airport. Ask Priscilla to email me your flight information. Who's coming with you?"

"Only Priscilla. The others will be visiting at various times."

"How's your mother?"

"She's in Middleburg. She says it's time for her to retire again. But she'll be coming to France for a couple of weeks with Nina and Adam."

"And the lovely Lilly? How's she?"

"She'll be coming, too, with her friend, who's more than a friend."

"What's all this?"

"He's a great guy. Our family doctor, actually. You'll like him."

"I'm looking forward to seeing everyone. Especially you. Why don't you come tomorrow?"

Careful, Charlotte thought and answered, "I'd like to. But I have an appointment. I want to set up a foundation for giving grants to retired dancers who want to start related businesses, like schools, physical therapy, costume design, et cetera."

"I like this idea. Can there be a French branch?"

"I'll ask the lawyers and let you know."

"I'll call you tomorrow at 5 p.m., your time."

They said goodbye, and Charlotte twirled around the tiny room, arms above her head. "Glitter is coursing through my veins! Is it seeping out?"

"Don't tell me his marriage plans fell through!"

"Yes, they did! Isn't it a crying shame? Let's celebrate with some of those chocolates you've got hidden around here."

Charles called right on time the next afternoon. "Was the meeting with your lawyers successful, *cherie*?"

"No problem having an international foundation. There are many ways to structure this. I have to meet with them again before I can leave for France."

"I've decided to come and get you. I leave on the first flight tomorrow for New York. I'll go with you to the lawyers and come back to Paris when you do."

"I'll be the one at the airport wearing a tutu. What plane are you on?"

"Air France, arriving at noon. I can't wait to see you."

"Me, too, you."

Charlotte grabbed a bag of Cheetos. She stuck her nose in it and breathed in the tantalizing scent before shifting into overdrive. Would Gani make a delicious boxed lunch tomorrow for her to have in the car for Charles? Would Priscilla make sure the guest room is perfect? Would Gani order a Porterhouse steak for dinner tomorrow night? Would Priscilla make an appointment with the hairdresser at ten tomorrow morning? Would Gani be sure to get Thomas' original English muffins and Irish butter for breakfast?

Charlotte headed for her bedroom. She did a rigorous fifteen-minute routine at the ballet barre to calm herself. Then she phoned Lilly.

"Sit down and hear my news."

"Tell me." Lilly was already seated in her living room, embroidery hoop in hand, monogramming a handkerchief for George.

"Charles will be here in less than twenty-four hours!"

"And Paulette? Is she coming too?"

"No. It's over!"

"You sound so happy. Am I missing something?"

"I never told you anything because it was too sad, but while I was in Normandy, I had hypnosis. After the second session, I realized I was totally crazy about Charles. This feeling grew in my heart day after day for over a week, and then I saw him. I was filled with joyous anticipation. And I could tell he was happy, too. I thought he'd been thinking about me, but that was when he told me he was going to remarry Paulette."

"That's a terrible beginning, but it's not over. And isn't it wonderful being in love?"

"It's better than any drug I've ever had."

"Charlotte, I'm so proud you kicked."

"It's thanks to Charles that I'm clean."

"We all owe him a big debt. You're a new person, and it's what you do next that counts."

They discussed the foundation, the book launch and the schedule for the coming season.

"How will you fit Charles into all this?"

"Dr. Kleper said whether or not you mean to change the world, you will, for better or worse. Now my life's finally unfolding as it should, and if I'm meant to be with Charles, I will be. I'm certain of that."

When the conversation ended, Charlotte walked over to her bedroom window, high above 71st Street, and looked south towards Midtown. Day was coming to a close. Lights were sparking the air. To her right, heavenly shades of lilac were mixing with red and gold in the western sky. Tomorrow would be the beginning of a new chapter. A *frisson* of excitement shimmied up her spine, and a smile lingered on her lips.

CPSIA information can be obtained
at www.ICGtesting.com
Printed in the USA
BVHW081734270519
549348BV00017B/1025/P

9 781623 860547